FREE INDEED SERIES

Book # 2 - Ephesians 6:12

FOR OUR STRUGGLE IS NOT AGAINST FLESH AND BLOOD...

A Novella

MARIA LENNON

1

Free Indeed Series
Book # 1 Set Free – ISBN 9781540707161
Book # 2 Our Struggle Is Not Against Flesh and Blood – ISBN 978-1542969765

By Maria Lennon
Most Bible scriptures are paraphrased.

Maria Lennon

.........., ...
Maria.conqueress@gmail.com

FREE INDEED SERIES

Book # 2 – FOR OUR STRUGGLE IS NOT AGAINST FLESH AND BLOOD

Ephesians 6:12 (KJV) For we wrestle not against flesh and blood, but against principalities, against powers, against the rulers of the darkness of this world, against spiritual wickedness in high places.

Acknowledgments:
I give thanks to the Lord, who gives us the confidence when He begins a good work in us, He will help us to perform and finish it until the day of Jesus Christ. (Phil. 1:6 paraphrased)

Thanks to my strongest supporters, my family, Tom, Esther, Tom V, JD, Tirzah, and Caleb.
Thanks to my friends Joyce and Al Bjorgum and their prayer friends.
My gratitude goes to Doyle and Becky McClung for your diligent edits and prayers.
Thanks to Lauren and Vicky, Leslie McCoy, and so many more prayer warriors who pray without ceasing for the Lord's will to be done here on earth as it is in heaven.

A group of teenagers sit on the lawn of the school grounds. Their subject books are open, and some write into their notebooks.

David, one of the boys, slams his book shut and gets up. "I think we studied enough. I for sure need to stop or my head is going to explode with information overload."

The twin girls get up and brush invisible grass off their clothing. Tina smiles, "Yes, I think we'll get a great score on our exam tomorrow. Thanks, guys." The twins leave.

Moriah puts her book and notebook inside her backpack. She gets up and swings her bag over one shoulder. "Thanks, that was an excellent study. I feel like I'm as ready as can be for our final tomorrow. I've got to run. It's already getting dark." She waves to her friends.

Her friends wave back. Some rise and leave, others stay.

*

Moriah rushes through the deserted town. Darkness lurks out of every corner. There is no traffic noise. It is like most everyone already is tucked in for the night. Moriah's sneakers make no sound. A cat jumps out of a dumpster and hides below a car. Moriah glances at the cat. She whispers. "Hello, Kitty."

Moriah looks at the time on her cell phone and hurries up a notch. She turns a corner into an even darker alley.

At the end of the passageway are three people quarreling, and having a brawl. After a few steps, Moriah realizes that those are not human but three hideous demonic creatures. She blows her hair out of her face and thinks to herself. 'What are they doing up here? Well, it doesn't matter. Lord, here I go!'

Light flashes from Moriah into the alley.

The demons stop cold in their tracks. Rage, one of the demons is so mad that he fumes. His eyes turn greenish. His creepy look focuses on Moriah.

Gossip is the other demon drooling while chattering, "I've got to tell the master about her. Oh, I must tell him as soon as possible."

Hate, the third demon sneers, "Now if that's not a real goody two shoes... Let's destroy her."

The three agree with menace and line up shoulder-to-shoulder blocking the alleyway, reaching their hands as to grab Moriah. Their talon claws gleam.

Moriah shakes her head and rolls her eyes. "Really? Watch this—." Moriah picks up her pace and leaps right through them.

WHOOSH. The demonic creatures disassemble, and parts of them fly around. They are super surprised and can't believe what just happened.

*

At the same time in hell, the green slimy walls of the cave-like throne room crumble. Rocks and dust fall from the ceiling.

Lucifer sits on his throne dressed in a red and black robe. He forms fireballs in his hand and throws them at the wispy dark minions and his demon servants.

The Minions crawl cowardly on the ground and along the shaking walls and ceiling. Hell rumbles like an earthquake.

Lucifer looks up. "What's happening up there?" And in a flash, he zooms himself up and out of hell into the alley. He appears right behind Moriah walking away.

Lucifer looks and sees his three demons disfigured from Moriah's walk-through. They are scrambling back into their shapes. He tilts his head looking at Moriah.

Lucifer asks his demons, "Did she do that? Who is she?"

Moriah doesn't turn around, but she says, "I can hear you. I tell you, you unclean brood, go back where you came from in the Lord's name."

And BAM, with a flash all of them, including Lucifer disappear from the alley. Only sulfur and dust clouds remain.

They end up back down in hell tumbling on the ground, scrambling up with cursing and shouting.

When Lucifer stands up, his face is crimson red, more than usual. He takes deep breaths to settle down. His skin also changes into a bronze color. He hollers. "What just happened?
I want to know right now."

Lucifer's underlings shrug their shoulders. They look at each other. No one knows anything.

Except Gossip appears to know, ploughing his way closer to Lucifer all pompous and drooling everywhere. "You should have seen her, Master. When she saw us blocking her way, she laughed and ran even faster to break through us. I've never seen anything like it. And the next thing I remember, you showed up."

Lucifer demands. "Get back, Gossip. You're not telling me anything new. Minions, get the principalities in warp speed. Go! There's got to be a reason for that earthling to have this kind of power."

The Minions and some servant demons scurry out of the room.

Lucifer paces back and forth and mumbles to himself. "If there's a manifestation like this up on earth, there's got to be something going on. Or else, why would she be messing with us?"

Out of the corner of his eyes, he sees Hate, Rage and Gossip trying to sneak away and heading for the tunnels to escape. He throws flaming ropes around each. They are stuck.

"Not you. You've got some explaining to do. It better be bad!" The three hang their heads and approach Lucifer's throne.

*

At the same time in South Korea, Vincent, an American, sits with crossed legs in the middle of an empty workout room. He remembers:

Vincent fights with Cho Ming outdoors in a lush green area with trees. They are wearing their traditional uniforms. Vincent's outfit is white with an embroidered golden eagle and a black belt.

Cho Ming, a South Korean man, wears his black uniform with a golden and red dragon embroidered on the back and the Yin Yang symbol on the left front.

They are circling each other and sometimes clash together, hands cupped and attack. Arms block. Then they kick and block. Right, left, right.

Vincent pins Cho Ming against a tree. "Why did you take Jasmine away from me? I wanted to marry her."

Cho Ming is dangerous, but a flicker of amusement in his eyes reveals that he is enjoying this. "It's the tradition of our ancestors that the Father chooses the groom for their daughters."

Cho Ming pushes Vincent away from him, and they duck again into fighting position.

"Because YOU asked him," replies Vincent.

They work a few hits, offense and defense. Pow, wow, pow.

"I've had my eye on her since she grew into a woman."

And again, they attack each other with their hands and arms real fast like pounding on a drum.

Vincent barks. "But she loves me. Not you and you know it."

Cho smirks at Vincent. "I am the man. She'll learn to love me."

Vincent gets mad. "Love isn't one-sided! It's giving and receiving. I know, love is something beautiful all by itself."

Unseen by the two opponents a dreadful Ninja Demon Warrior-Foe appears out of thin air. His focus is on Vincent and slips into his body. Vincent's eyes turn blood red.

Cho Ming belittles Vincent. "It's not like you invented love."

Being under the power of the Warrior-Foe, Vincent grows furious. He turns and kicks Cho Ming so hard, that he stumbles and falls to the ground. Vincent jumps on top of him. Driven by madness from the dark power within, he curves his hand for a deathblow at Cho Ming's throat.

Right at this moment, Vincent's Cross Pendant slips out of his uniform and swings above Cho Ming's face.

The Cross sparkles in the sunlight and into Vincent's vision. Vincent shakes himself and relaxes his hand. He releases Cho Ming and gets up.

Warrior-Foe slips out of Vincent's body. He is very confused. He points his finger at Vincent. "You'll be mine… One Day, soon." And puff, he vanishes in an instant.

Vincent turns and walks away from Cho Ming. He looks at his hands wondering what just happened.

"I thought we were fighting for Jasmine?" Cho Ming calls.

Vincent freezes and turns half way around. "The fight was between you and me. Not ever FOR

Jasmine. Be happy that you live." With that, he walks off.'

Vincent comes back to reality and tries to shake away his painful memories. He sighs and gets up, walking around the room. He talks to himself: "I don't know why I got so uncontrollably furious, and I don't want this ever to happen again. I love fighting, but I don't want to hurt anyone. It's a good thing to leave everything behind and go home for a while."

Warrior Foe enters the room in his spirit form. His grimace is hideous, and he laughs to himself.

Vincent bows his head in prayer. "Creator, I present my life to you. Please, I need you to show me how to do the right thing with my life."

The words of Vincent's prayer turn to gold as soon as he speaks them. They rise into the air. Warrior Foe catches each one of them and eats them and burps loudly. "I already have plans for you and you'll be mine in no time."

Vincent turns to the door and caresses the ancient blessing hanging on the doorframe. Then he walks out and closes the door behind himself. And PUFF, Warrior Foe disappears.

*

Mr. Hanes, a pleasant 81-year-old gentleman, sits in his wheelchair on the porch of his little home. He enjoys flipping through pages of a photo album. He chuckles at a picture even though he is listening to Moriah's story from last evening.

Moriah finishes telling him what happened in the alley last night. "If I didn't know any better, I'd say, someone is in trouble, or I wouldn't have seen these demons. I hope to find out who it is that needs help."

Mr. Hanes pats Moriah's hand. "You will, dear, the Lord always leads you in the right direction. And I'm here to support you." Mr. Hanes looks at Moriah and nods with encouragement.

Moriah smiles. She fills a bird feeder with seeds and hangs the feeder up on a tree. Once done, she flattens the empty birdseed bag and reads the writing. She shows it to Mr. Hanes. "Look here, Mr. Hanes. There is a photo contest; you can send up to three of your best bird photos and win $ 500. — and one hundred pounds of bird seed."

"Get out. Let me see." He takes the bag and reads.

Moriah gets inside the house and in a flash comes back out with a tripod and a camera. She sets it up close to Mr. Hanes. "How's that?"

Mr. Hanes looks through the camera and fiddles with it. "Wonderful, just right."

"You know, David would love to print any new photos you take. The deadline is in a week."

Mr. Hanes smiles at Moriah. "All right, I'll keep my eyes open for the best shots. I'm so glad you and your friends gave me this camera for my 81-year-old birthday. Thanks… Oh, before I forget. Vincent called from South Korea. He's coming back to town soon. He's tying up loose ends as we speak." Moriah is surprised. "I thought he'd stay over there for life. He'll have stories to tell, Mr. Hanes."

Mr. Hanes snickers to himself and grabs his camera. "And I'll have one more good chess partner as well unless he forgot how to play."

Moriah picks up her backpack and turns to leave. "I've got to go to school, Mr. Hanes. We have this huge exam. It's the last one. After it, we are on vacation. See you tonight to tuck you into bed."

"Thank you, Moriah. Have a good day."

Moriah walks to the end of the porch and jumps over the fence. She walks in the back of the neighborhood yards along the flowers and trees, taking a deep breath of their fragrances.

Moriah skips along the path. She hears two people argue loudly. She slows down and peeks through the bushes and observes.

A young man quarrels with a young woman.

The young brunette woman grips the man's shirt by the buttons with both hands. His shirt slips out of his pants. She shakes him with all her strength.

The young man holds the woman's wrist and one shoulder trying to get her off him.

The young female screams through her tears: "I don't believe anything anymore coming from you."

The young man tries to calm her down: "But honey, I love you so much. I was working—"

"Don't you honey me," she yells at him angrily.

Just watching distresses Moriah. She takes a step forward to get a better look. She sees not only the young man and young woman fighting with each other, but she also sees into the spirit realm. The demon of Strife and his cousin Anger slide in and out of the young man and the young woman. They are influencing the young couple and drive them to madness.

Moriah rolls her eyes and straightens up and steps closer.
"Why, I should have guessed it, spirits of strife."

The young man is now angry: "Let's call it off then. You are too demanding and selfish, and like that ALL the time."

A clue for the woman: "See! You never loved me-" She cries.

Moriah is out of the bushes in the open and walks toward the couple. While she walks, she speaks under her breath in a demanding whisper and directly to Strife and Anger. "Strife and Anger I bind your power, and you two leave right now, this minute, in the name of the Lord."

17

Strife and Anger freeze half in and out of the young couple's bodies. Their faces turn to frowns. They stare at Moriah and then they take off with protests.

Strife whines: "What's SHE doing here? Spoiling our fun, AGAIN." Anger chimes in: "I'm going to get even with her one day, and then for the worst-"

WHOOSH - they are gone.

Moriah reaches the couple and says: "Excuse me, please. I couldn't help overhearing that you have such a difficult time."

The couple looks at each other very confused, having forgotten the reason for the fight since Strife and Anger are gone now. The young woman lets go of the man's clothing and wipes her tears with her sleeves. She straightens his shirt and then her dress. "You can say that again." She replies.

The young man tugs his shirt back into his pants. "Yes, something was difficult. I just don't remember what."

The birds are chirping and bees are buzzing around. It feels like peace is back.

Moriah continues: "I can see you are very much in love. But a fight isn't a solution. I know lots of other ways to show love.

The young woman agrees. "You are right. I don't know what has gotten into me."

The young man shakes his head. "Honestly I don't know either what happened."

The young woman takes a step toward the young man and puts her head on his chest in remorse. "Could you please forgive me?"

The young man wraps his arms around her. He is relieved. "Oh yes, honey. And please forgive me also. Let's talk about what just happened." She replies quickly, "No. Let's not. It feels like it was a nightmare."

Moriah steps away and toward the fence and waves. "You two are sweet. I wish all differences in the world could be worked out that natural."

The woman asks her, "Could you stay for a cup of coffee?

Moriah shakes her head. "Maybe another time."
The young man lifts his hand to wish her good bye. "All right. Have a beautiful day." The woman agrees. "Yes. And thank you."

Moriah nods her head and ducks to go back through the bushes. "You're welcome." Then she whispers, "Thank you, Lord."

*

Lucifer sits on his throne. A multitude of demons are coming from several tunnels to stand before him and reporting one by one the cases they are working.

Amongst the closest waiting in line is Hate, in his green, orange and purple colors. He mumbles to himself. "I hate reporting day. Look at them all, shaking and afraid. No wonder we never won any of the wars. No one is going anywhere but down here." He is fuming green bubbles out of his mouth.

Killer-demon is next in line in front of Hate. He wears a long trench coat and an oversized brimmed hat down to his eyes. He sneers at Hate. When killer-demon sees the green bubbles come out of Hate's mouth, he makes sure that none of it splatters on his coat. Then, he quickly turns his focus back to Lucifer so that he wouldn't miss his turn.

Lucifer waves another reporting demon away. He shakes his head. "Get out of my sight. Do something worse." He mutters to himself, "Forever has become even longer with you. GO!"

The demon steps away, when passing fellow demons, they sneer and ridicule him.

Lucifer throws a rain of fireballs at the demons for them to shut up. The demon disappears in the exit tunnel.

Killer-Demon steps forward. He shouts with great pomp. "I've been through lands around the Globe. Wherever I found a dark soul open for me, I was there. I possessed humans. Some of them turned serial killers, like Jack the Ripper."

Lucifer shrugs his shoulders. "So what? Any low ranked demon can do that. People have murdered all the way back since Cain. This isn't anything new. Now, if you'd ever get a leader of a country blood thirsty, then hundreds or thousands of innocent lives will die. My advice, work harder. Get a grip on the leaders of the earthlings and pollute them. THAT will expand my kingdom."

Killer-Demon contradicts. "Your Highness, you must have forgotten that I worked on

Hitler, and all the other masses in other countries which the leaders and their followers buried in mass graves." He gets closer to Lucifer and continues. "The earthlings still haven't found some of the mass graves." He stands upright and his chest gets bigger. "These are my works, and to the leaders you speak of, yes, I'm instrumental with the terrorists. I hope age hasn't eaten some of your memory."

Lucifer doesn't like Killer-Demon and the way he talks to him. "You've got an answer to everything now, don't you?"

While Lucifer and Killer-Demon converse back and forth, Hate's relatives, Rage, Fear and Anger get antsy. Strife and Gossip are with them in a cluster. And behind all of them stands Warrior-Foe, high and untouchable. He doesn't bother looking at any of the demonic underlings.

Gossip is the most impatient of them all drooling all over himself. Bursting to get a turn, Gossip pushes forward. Strife thrusts Gossip continually back into his place. Gossip tries to cut again. Strife turns and unfolds his torn slimy wings and holds his hands as if he wants to strangle Gossip.

Lucifer's eyes blaze orange fire between them. They look up in shock and get back in line as they were before. Except, now Gossip stays put, however, it is very hard for him to control himself.

Killer-Demon is finished stating his case and salutes Lucifer and bows. "Yes, your Majesty. As you wish, your Majesty."

Lucifer is frustrated and looks bored. Killer-Demon leaves carrying his head and shoulders up high.

Strife steps forward. "Holder of Evil. By ever working strife to honor my name, I have come across a male weakling who is most pliable to my influence. And my cousin Rage could take over and possess this weak soul.

Lucifer rolls his eyes. "So what?"

Strife puffs himself up. "I've heard of the failure of my cousins Anger and Rage… In the alley with a particular girl-" He looks toward Hate and Rage with victory.

Lucifer taps his finger on his armrest. "Get on with it, or you're going to be fried."

Strife grins. "Here is the juicy part. I brought your sore subject into the picture—"

Rage steps out of line passing Gossip and flaring a mad look at Strife. And Anger also leaps forward. They look like they are going to tear each other up right there.

Rage shouts. "Your working is feeble, Strife, all you do is go back and forth and bring the humans to argue. I worked that man hard and often. I finally got him to the point where he lost ALL control."

Anger puffs in between them. "Don't you just leave me out cousin Rage, I did most of the groundwork, and because of that you were able to slip inside the person."

Lucifer keeps looking from one to the other. "So? And why should that interest me more than all the million times you have done that before? And what exactly is MY SORE subject? Tell me."

Gossip jumps forward drooling so much that slime runs down his chest. "Move out of my way you brood. If it weren't for me to tell everyone about everything, the information wouldn't have grown like wildfire. Your sore subject, goody two shoes Moriah, has a circle of friends. We can stir them up against her."

When Lucifer hears the name Moriah, he sits up straight. "Moriah! That troublemaker. I despise humans with a gift from the Bright Side." He thinks and talks to himself quietly. "There is no antidote, except for sin, and we still need to clarify why she had so much power in the alley."

Lucifer motions for silence straining his head for answers. Then he points the finger at the five: Strife, Anger, Rage, Hate and Gossip, and directs them to the side.

"Wait over there. Quietly! We need to plan this effectively." The five get out of the way and slump down with their character attitudes making sure they don't touch each other.

Lucifer waves the next in line. "Next! Well hello. What brings YOU to me?" Warrior-Foe steps proudly forward with his head lifted high. He rests the back of his hand on his hip revealing a shiny golden sword set with precious stones.

His voice is deep. "I have many servants among the earthlings, most of them live to fight and die fighting. More power to you

Lucifer. One raised interest in me; Marvelous attention, very detailed and precise, a rare talent, he is."

Warrior-Foe poses in front of Lucifer, but also parades back and forth in front of the gaping demons watching him. He evidently enjoys having an audience. Looking around he continues, "That one's moved back to his hometown in America. And he teaches ancient Martial arts. He is almost my own and ready to win others over to our side."

Lucifer lifts his hand up for silence. The geysers sizzle and the walls crumble. Lucifer stands up. He looks at Gossip. "One earthling? Gossip, you know about this?"

Gossip jumps up and gets closer slobbering even more. "Of course, I know! Nothing escapes me. He is talking about a long lost friend of Moriah's."

Lucifer claps his hands one time. "Aha. Is that so? Now that's the bad news I wanted to hear."

Gossip continues. "Another one of her friends is a student in the Fight school."

Lucifer is pleased. "So, I've got a plan: Everyone, be yourselves. Continue doing what you have started. AND KEEP RANKS. You've got to let the little ones prepare the way." He walks around the group and gives each a stern look. "Gossip first stirs them up. That way they will get into arguments, and that's when Hurt and Strife show up to raise the stakes. Anger follows, so be ready to strike at the right time. That's when you have your turn, Rage, hassle everyone so much that they'll lose control over themselves. I want to see ALL of the earthlings fall. Show me what you've got. I might even do some fieldwork myself."

Warrior-Foe looks down on Strife, Anger, Rage, Hurt and Gossip. They look at him and Lucifer. He shakes his head. "Oh brother, if you say so."

Lucifer raises his eyebrows and puts his hands on his hips. "Get to work… NOW."

They scramble to get away from Lucifer and out the exit tunnel. Only Warrior-Foe takes each step with assurance, knowing he will pursue his agenda even without these detestable demonic beings.

*

Moriah walks happily along the roadside. She stops at a house and rings the doorbell.

Rosina, the mother of one of Moriah's summer jobs only opens the door a crack to see who is outside. She looks like she was crying.

Moriah tries to cheer Rosina up and speaks in a singsong voice. "All my finals are done, Rosina, can you believe it? Summer vacation has opened the doors for me. Can I play with Bella?"

Rosina turns ashen, "Oh, Moriah, I forgot to call you. Bella had an accident, and she's in the hospital."

"What kind of an accident? Could I visit her?"

Rosina hesitates. She looks scared leaning back listening inside the house. All is quiet. She breathes hard and takes a few moments to answer. "Well, she is ill. The hospital sent me home to get some rest. I'll stop by there again on my way to work. Maybe wait a day or two to visit her. I'll keep you posted on her condition. Bye now."

Rosina wants to shut the door, but Moriah scoots her foot inside the door frame and holds on to Rosina's arm. Rosina flinches by the touch of Moriah. And with a quick motion, Moriah pulls back the loose sleeve of Rosina's blouse. Rosina's arm is all bruised up looking like fingerprints.

"I'm sorry, I didn't know. Please, tell me what's going on. How ill is Bella? What does she have?"

Rosina shrugs her shoulders. Tears build up in her eyes. "She's had an accident. She is in intensive care at St. John's hospital."

Moriah is irritated by memories rushing in from times past she has seen abused women before with their bruises. Moriah isn't sure and treads carefully, wanting to get a better answer. "Did she have an accident like you had on your arm? You know you can get help if someone abuses you."

Rosina shakes her head violently and looks at Moriah's foot in the door. Moriah steps back from the door and Rosina shuts it immediately.

While Moriah stands there and thinks about her next step, she casts a glance at the windows of the house and sees Gene, Bella's dad lurking through a curtain. Thoughts stream through her mind. 'What a coward, he doesn't even have the guts to come out and talk with me. Something is wrong with this picture. I better go and see how Bella is doing.'

Moriah looks at the window once again. Gene is gone, only the curtain moves. She takes quick steps and heads down the street.

*

Later, Moriah opens the door to Bella's hospital room. Everything is quiet. Bella is hooked on to all kinds of lifeline instruments, which beep rhythmic. She has small oxygen hoses going into her nose. A dripper is attached to Bella's wrist.

Moriah steps inside as quiet as she can. She is scared for the seven-year-old girl, who lies in bed so still as if there's no life within her. Her head is bandaged but shows swellings and bruises on the exposed face and her right arm.

Moriah sits on a chair very close to the bed. She holds Bella's slender, small hand on her own, then puts it back on the bedcover carefully. She gets up and kisses Bella's forehead and walks to the window.

She cries silently and whispers a prayer to the Lord. "Oh, Father. Who could hurt this precious girl so badly? God, your Word says, if anyone makes one of these little ones stumble, it's better for him to have a Millstone around his neck and be cast into the sea. I sure feel like finding the one responsible and do it myself... Bella is one of the sweetest girls I know... Please let her live."

Bella stirs. "Ahhmmm..."

Moriah wipes her tears again and spins around. She rushes to the bed and touches Bella's shoulder. Moriah's necklace dangles from her neck. The pendant has three flames and below the words: PRAYER ABLAZE.

Moriah coos to Bella. "Bella...?"

Bella breathes visibly deeper and opens her eyes. She smiles faintly. It takes her a few attempts to speak. "Moriah... My Mom?"

Moriah is so happy that Bella is conscious. With great effort, she tries to sound calm. "Oh, Bella! I'm so glad you woke up. Your mom is okay. She needed rest and will stop by again before she goes to work. I thought I could stay with you for a while."

Bella looks around the walls of her room and all the beeping and buzzing instruments. "Am I in a hospital?"

"Yes, you are. The doctors and nurses will make you all better."

Bella smiles again. "Good, I hurt everywhere."

Moriah's tears well up again. Suddenly she hears a whisper of wings behind herself and looks.

The Guardian of Bella, an illuminated angel, stands transparently behind Bella's headboard. The bed and wall do not limit his presence to protect Bella. He signals with his head toward the large window to the hallway.

Moriah turns her head and sees Bella's dad looking through the window. He just stands there, hesitating to come inside the room.

Moriah whispers. "Bella, your dad is outside the room. Should I leave?"

Bella takes on a frantically scared look but doesn't move her head. She closes her eyes immediately, and says, "Stay. Don't tell him I'm awake." She lies motionless.

Moriah is stunned. Guardian puts a protective arm around Bella.

Gene is about 47 years old. He enters the room but leaves the door open. He looks at Bella and Moriah. "Did she wake up yet?"

Moriah presses her lips together and looks at Bella and shrugs her shoulders.

Gene is in a bad mood and his face changes into an angry grimace. Rage lurks out of Gene and changes colors from black to red to orange and dark purple. He pounds on Gene's head.

Moriah sees the whole supernatural scene. She is speechless.

Gene struggles from within not to do anything hasty. He turns from being timid to confused, then angry then back to confused again in short timespans.

Guardian sparks a gleam from his eyes toward Rage and ZAP, he hides in Gene and holds still.

Gene huffs. "I saw you through the window. You were talking."

Moriah answers carefully to calm Gene down. "So… I was praying. If you like to join me in prayer, that would be lovely. I'm praying that your little girl is going to make it.

Gene shudders and glances again at Bella. He softens. "No, I can't… I've got to go. Eh…

33

go to… work. See you. With that, he leaves in a hurry.

Rage accompanies him steadily. He turns sideways and makes awful Raspberry sounds toward Guardian and Moriah.

Moriah gets up and closes the door. Anger appears and sneaks up behind Moriah. He waits for his chance to get a grip on her. She is not aware of him. But Guardian flashes a stern look at Anger, and he retreats defiantly.

Bella opens her eyes again. "Thank you, Moriah. I didn't mean for you to lie for me."

Moriah sits down at her bedside and smiles with calmness. "Don't worry. It wasn't a lie. I've been praying the whole time when you were unconscious."

Bella sighs. "You know, I love my daddy. He is the only daddy I have."

Moriah pads Bella's hand gently. "I know, Bella."

Bella continues. "Sometimes he gets so angry, then he just hits Mom, and I don't know why." Bella cries softly.

Moriah tries to comfort her. She also has teary eyes. "I'm sorry. That must be hard."

"I made cookies the way you showed me one day. I put them in a pile on one of our best plates. When I went to give him one, I fell over his work boots, dropped the plate, and it broke. The cookies flew everywhere." Bella cries with the memory.

Moriah bites her lips and softly wipes Bella's face with a tissue. "Shh, shh. It's okay. Don't cry about that plate. Breaking things happens to the best. It was an accident.

Bella looks at Moriah. "But, I broke Dad's favorite plate. It's my fault. He got angry and then he started to hit me and didn't stop. Mom tried to help, and I saw Dad push her away so hard, that she fell and didn't get up. Now I am afraid of him."

Moriah gives Bella another tissue and takes one for herself. They both cry. When they calm down again, Moriah takes Bella's hand and kisses it.

"I'm sorry Bella. I want you to know your mom is okay. You are way more important than the plate. There is no one like you, or it wouldn't be you. A plate is easily replaced. But you, Bella, can NOT be replaced. You are special, and there is only one of you out there in the world."

Bella smiles. "Thanks, Moriah… I'm hungry."

Guardian nods. Moriah straightens up and pushes the call button for the Nurse. Then she walks over to the sink and washes her face. Just as she wipes it dry, a nurse comes in and smiles at Bella. "Well, look at you little tree climber. You are lucky, that you are alive, falling from a tall tree. Get well first before you climb on one of those again, okay?"

Bella smiles weakly at the nurse.

Moriah changes the subject. "Bella says she's hungry." Bella nods.

The nurse checks the vital signs and chimes. "Hungry is good. I'll fetch some soup and pudding for you, precious." With that, she leaves.

Moriah wets a washcloth and wrings it out. "Now we know what people think what happened to you. I'll talk to your mom, and see what she has to say. Good?"

Bella agrees with relief. She asks. "Please, could you stay with me a while longer? I don't want to be alone."

Moriah wipes Bella's forehead with the damp washcloth. "Of course, I'll stay, until your mother is back. But you know, you are not alone, ever. Your Guardian Angel protects you." Moriah takes her necklace off and gives it to Bella.

Bella looks at the praying hands pendant and smiles. "Cool, I like it."

Moriah puts the necklace around Bella's neck. "This is a reminder that you are not alone and to pray anytime, you think about praying."

Bella nods and touches the necklace.

The nurse comes in with a tray of food and drink and props it in front of Bella. She opens the pudding and spoon-feeds Bella.

*

Meanwhile at Mr. Hanes House is a small party. Vincent plays chess with Mr. Hanes. There are only a few pieces remaining on the chessboard. Mr. Hanes is enjoying the game.

David, the 20-year-old geek, is busy getting paper plates, napkins and sodas lined up on the Kitchen counter, which overlooks the living room. He decides to take off his blue ski hat and stuffs it in his back pants pocket. He runs his fingers through his hair. "Anyone wants to drink soda with me?"

"We'll take soda, David. Vincent looks like he's losing the game."

Vincent grins. He is relaxed. His facial features are soft and handsome. He seems almost like a different person than when he was in Korea.

The doorbell chimes. David puts two sodas next to his friends and goes to open the door. Diane, Moriah's 28-year-old friend, stands in the doorframe all smiles in her hot pink and purple outfit. She carries two large pizza boxes.

Mr. Hanes stretches from his wheelchair to see who it is. "Diane! Thank God you're here. I was wondering what happened."

Diane walks into the house and puts the Pizza boxes on the table. "Hi, I thought I'd never get out of work today."

David closes the door and helps to get the pizza onto the paper plates.

Diane continues. "And not only that, it seems like everywhere I went, stuff happened.

Like there was this protest in the middle of Broadway. Who protests on the main road at the time of the heaviest business traffic? I almost gave up, and I thought I should just go home and call it a day."

She takes off her coat and hangs it on an empty chair.

Mr. Hanes looks at her and winks his eye. "I'm glad you made it and are here."

Vincent chimes in. "Me too. I'm starving."

Diane is delighted to see Vincent and goes to him. Vincent gets up, and they hug. "It's so good to see you, Diane."

Diane takes a step back and checks Vincent out. "Hello, Vincent. Wow, you turned out to be good looking after all."

Vincent doesn't let go of Diane's one hand and glances at her openly from head to toes. "I don't know what you mean, but I have to admit, you look great, Diane, quite gorgeous, I must say."

Diane laughs and pulls her hand back. She teases. "Thanks, you silly."

Mr. Hanes moves a piece on the chessboard. "Checkmate! Let's eat while it is still warm. Help yourselves."

Vincent shakes his head looking at the board. "I thought I had you. I've got to brush up on my skills. Good game, H."

David slides a plate with pizza in front of Mr. Hanes. He has three more plates each with a piece of pizza and hands it out to his friends. They take it and sit down and eat.

Diane asks, "Where is Moriah? I thought she'd be here already."

Mr. Hanes informs Diane. "She called a little while ago. She's visiting a friend at the hospital and will come by later. Vincent, tell us some of your adventures in Korea. We'd love to hear about them."

*

Moriah is in a private waiting room at the hospital. There is a couch and a coffee table. The chairs are lined up along the wall and on one of them sits Bella's young mother, Rosina. She is crying her eyes out. She holds a bunch of crumpled up tissues in her hand. She wipes the unceasing tears rolling down her thin cheeks. Her black hair hangs all stringy over her face.

Moriah paces the floor in frustration. Anger paces right behind her, ready to pop inside her if there is a chance. She doesn't notice. "Thank God that Bella will be okay."

Rosina nods. "Hmm." She blows her nose and sighs.

Moriah stops in front of Rosina and asks kindly. "What are you going to do now?"

Rosina lifts one of her shoulders. "Maybe I will put up a gate guard, or I just have to be more around her, that she'll not fall downstairs anymore."

Moriah is shocked with that answer. "What are you talking about? First, it's a tree, now stairs? You know that neither is true, and you know the reason why Bella is in the condition she's in right now."

Rosina stares at Moriah and thinks of another excuse. She even stops crying. "How would you know? I… I was there."

Moriah grabs Rosina's shoulders with both hands looking straight into her eyes. "Think about it, Rosina, and face the truth. I don't know how many years your husband abused you physically, and somehow no one found out. Now, it's your precious little girl. She's in pretty bad shape."

Rosina barely breathes being scared. "The doctor said she'd be all right."

Moriah let's go of Rosina's shoulders and steps back. "Yeah, this time her body will heal, but what about next time? Or even worse, what about her soul, or what about her fragile little mind? How many years has she been watching you get beaten up? Do you know what that does to a young person? Do You?"

Rosina is shaken up by Moriah's words. "I… I…"

Moriah continues, "Children have this protection of the Lord, and they will bounce back many times. But not if it happens so often, that the memory grinds itself inside their hearts and soul, so deep that only a miracle can heal them completely."

Rosina wants to say something. "But—"

Moriah shakes her head not wanting to be interrupted. "… She might turn out to be afraid for the rest of her life. Every time someone raises their voice, or whatever that is that will trigger her memory, she will be afraid. If not you, who else will protect her?"

Rosina sobs again. "Okay… She didn't fall down the stairs or the tree, but he said he is not ever going to do that again. Seeing her suffer made him feel so very sorry."

Moriah throws up her hands. She steps closer to Rosina. "And you believe that? Again? Didn't he tell you that every time after he had beaten you up?"

Rosina is cornered. "But it will be different this time."

Moriah calms herself down. She talks in a somber and quiet tone. "No, Rosina, it won't. Your husband needs serious help from someone other than you. You and Bella need to be in a safe house, or whatever is out there to help you."

Rosina shakes her head. "He will be terribly mad if I did that."

Moriah looks sternly at Rosina. "See. That's exactly what I'm saying. Anytime you or Bella do something that aggravates him, he will turn aggressive again. And most of the times you don't even know what triggers it. It depends on his mood."

Rosina gets up from her chair. "I want to go home now and take Bella with me."

Moriah disagrees. "Bella is in good hands here. The Doctors will release her when she is ready. Can I give you a ride home?"

Rosina walks to the door. "No thanks. I came with my car." She opens the door and steps out of the room.

Moriah admonishes her. "Think about what I said. I will help you as much as I can… you don't have to go through this alone. Please let me know if you need help."

Rosina hesitates for a moment. "I'll think about it. Good night."

"Good night, Rosina. Call me anytime."

Rosina throws her tissues into the trash before she closes the door. Moriah stares at the closed door and shakes her head. Anger takes his fingers and tries to reach into the back of Moriah's head to scramble her thoughts. But he has no success.

Moriah walks out of the room and walks towards Bella's room. She passes a large window that overlooks the almost empty parking lot. Something draws Moriah to look outside. She sees Rosina in a dark corner of the hospital building leaning on the wall and then she slides down and ends up in a fetal position and crying.

Moriah sighs and continues her way to Bella's room. She looks through the window and sees Bella sound asleep and her Guardian Angel all around her. Moriah whispers, "Thank you."

She makes her way out of a side exit of the hospital. The night seems darker than usual. Moriah looks both ways before crossing the parking lot. There is no sign of Rosina. But somehow, Moriah has a creepy feeling like she is being watched. However, she doesn't see anyone.

Across the parking lot, Gene is hiding behind bushes and watches Moriah's every move. Lots of cigarette butts are on the ground. Gene takes one more puff of the one cigarette he is smoking and tosses it on the ground to the others already there. He steps on the butt and follows Moriah.

Rage rides Gene like he owns him.

Moriah hears someone behind her and walks faster. She reaches an open meadow at the park and turns around one more time, still seeing no one. She walks through the park.

Gene stops behind a car. He wants to remain hidden.

Rage initiates Gene's thinking and also his words. They both move their lips synchronized. "One day for sure, I'm going to get you." Rage continues alone. "Yeah, one day when she's going to invite me into her mind. Then we can tear her up into a million pieces. Real good. No, real bad. Hehehehe."

*

Moriah arrives at Mr. Hanes' home and goes inside. The friends, Mr. Hanes, Diane, Vincent, and David, are done eating pizza and enjoy each other's company. When they see Moriah, they are happy that she arrived before the party was over.

Mr. Hanes waves at Moriah. "Come have pizza and soda. Or whatever you like. And look, Vincent is here."

Vincent gets up and gives Moriah a little hug. "Hey, girl, you look gorgeous, you know that don't you?"

Moriah grins and slaps Vincent's shoulder. "You charmer. You always were a charmer. Nice

46

to see you, Vincent. I'm glad you're back in the States. Boy, I'm starved." She goes to the pizza box and puts two slices of pizza onto a paper plate.

David gives Mr. Hanes a package. "Here, that's from all of us. Moriah told us that you'd need it, like tomorrow."

Mr. Hanes rubs his hands together like a little boy. He looks at everyone and then opens the present. It is a box of photo paper and a photo album. "You guys! That's super. Just what I needed. Did she also tell you about the picture contest, David?"

David laughs. "Well, of course, she did. And I do have time to print them out, and we can send them into the contest. I've seen your pictures. There are some beautiful shots, and you have a good chance to win this competition."

Mr. Hanes is happy. Vincent nods his head. "It's good to be back home with you all. I don't know why I didn't come sooner."

Mr. Hanes waves everyone together. "Come, let's take a group shot. David, can you take one with you in the photo?"

David grabs the digital camera and props it up opposite from Mr. Hanes. "Of course I can. It's easy. Everyone, get together in a cluster. I'll join you in a flash."

David guides Diane to stand next to Mr. Hanes, and Vincent stands behind Mr. Hanes. Moriah stands next to Diane. He sets the self-timer and runs to Mr. Hanes side.

CLICK. David runs back to the camera and shows everyone the photo and gives the camera back to Mr. Hanes. He takes it, and after looking at the picture, he puts the camera back into the pouch. "I like it."

Diane sits down on a chair. "Vincent, tell me about your Martial Arts School. Do you have a lot of students?"

Vincent shakes his head. "Not yet, but we have a few students. It is a good beginning."

David is excited. "I'm one of his students. I take Tae Kwon Do classes starting tomorrow.

Diane loves the idea. "Can I come and take a look?"

Vincent enjoys his friends. "Sure, the classes are all day long. Some at lunchtime, most of them are in the evening, and our newest one is every morning for Thai Chi practices."

Diane asks. "Is that the one people find relaxing and strengthening at the same time?"

"Yes, that's the one. And all over the world, people know it as relaxing. But translated it literarily means "Great ultimate fist." Originally it was intended for fighting."

Mr. Hanes makes a fist and nods to himself. "Well, I certainly could use a great ultimate fist. Wow… powerful."

Diane gets up and takes the paper plates and soda cans from the table and off everyone's hands. "So? How long were you in Korea?"

Vincent answers. "Over seven years. I loved being there. I studied the culture and the foods and trained in different forms of Martial arts. That's how I ended up spending most of my time learning one after another discipline of fighting."

Mr. Hanes is curious. "Did you meet a beautiful girl over there?"

Vincent hesitates with the answer. He glances over at Diane and back to Mr. Hanes.

"Well, maybe… Maybe that's why I'm back home. I'm almost getting too old to marry."

Everyone laughs. Mr. Hanes teases. "Maybe, when you're a hundred years old, then you might be too old to get married.

Diane joins the conversation. "You're not old at all, just right." She lifts her eyebrows and smiles at Vincent.

David says, "Diane, you don't have a boyfriend either, do you?" He looks at her expecting an answer.

Diane waves David's remark off. "Hush, you. When can we see your school, Vincent?"

Vincent welcomes the change of subject. "Come and visit Tuesday night. I have an open house from 7 until 8:30 for the Community. Of course, you can come other days as well—"

Diane is excited. "No, Tuesday is perfect. I'll go with Mr. Hanes, and he can watch the Thai Chi classes. And I'm going to watch David… Moriah, are you doing anything Tuesday evening?"

Moriah chews on her pizza. She takes a sip of her soda to wash it down. "Well, I don't have any plans, but I'm not into fighting at all. I'll join you for the company. I hardly ever have time to go places with you."

Vincent nods. "All right it's a date then… eh, a plan."

*

Later on at night, Moriah helps Mr. Hanes to get comfortable in his bed. She puts the wheelchair close to the bed, in case Mr. Hanes has to get up at night. She puffs up the pillows and puts them behind his back.

"What's wrong Moriah? You've hardly said a word all night. You told me Bella is going to be all right. Isn't she?"

Moriah lays his Bible into his hands and turns on the night lamp. She looks at him. "Well, yes. It's her dad. I'm so mad at him, and I know that's not like me to get mad, and so I get even madder."

Mr. Hanes take Moriah's hand and pats it. "Getting mad or angry at someone isn't helping anyone."

"I know Mr. Hanes. I just don't know what to do."

Mr. Hanes sighs as he remembers. "I've seen a lot of people in my life, including myself get mad and angry at someone, and usually it doesn't stop there. It's a living thing, and sooner or later it takes over, and people lose control of their actions, and others get hurt."

Moriah interrupts. "That might be the case with Mr. Smith, not me."

Mr. Hanes glances at Moriah, knowing that she is hurt. "You're right. That's not like you. Hm… the good book says, where envy and strife are, there is confusion and every evil work. I hope a solution shows up soon before more damage gets done."

Moriah agrees. "Definitely! A solution should be around the corner, because I'm confused. None of us want 'every evil' work in our lives. Something is boggling my mind and I just can't figure out what it means."

Moriah sits down in Mr. Hanes' wheelchair. He is very attentively. "Tell me about it. Maybe we can figure it out together?"

Moriah gathers her thoughts. "Remember, I told you about the bunch of demons in the alley last night?" She looks at Mr. Hanes. He nods his head. Moriah continues. "Today, when I was in the hospital, I saw an unclean spirit, looking like someone who is consumed by rage, messing with Bella's dad."

Mr. Hanes nods. "Sounds like you're on a new divine assignment, or you wouldn't be able to see into the spirit world."

"Right. But the job isn't clear to me at all. Oh, I forgot, your neighbors had an argument which was stirred on by Anger and Strife."

Mr. Hanes shrugs his shoulders. "Write it all down. And take it one day at a time. The Lord is in control, and you're doing His bidding. Watch and pray always."

Moriah gets up. "Thanks, Mr. Hanes, I'll do that. Who knows, I might even be able to use my notes for the coming schoolyear."

"Good girl. Now, go home and get a good night's sleep."

Moriah walks to the door and turns the ceiling light off. "Good night, Mr. Hanes. Sleep well." She gets her things and leaves Mr. Hanes' house.

Outside she jumps down the step at the front door. Her backpack hangs over one shoulder. She crosses the quiet road.

WHOOSH. Something moves behind a bush. Moriah looks twice, but there is nothing. WHOOSH again. It is Lucifer behind Moriah. He rubs his hands with glee.

Anger and Rage give each other the 'high five.'

A WHISPER of wings and Illumina, Moriah's Guardian Angel stands tall in the street.

Moriah sees him and immediately she knows something is up. She looks directly at Illumina. "Please, tell me what's going on?"

Illumina brightens up. "You know when you and I speak, the whole universe can hear every word and also, the dark ones can hear our words. Therefore, give heed and keep the secrets of the Lord in your heart. Your silence is sometimes of vital importance. And rest assured you'll know what to do when the time comes."

Moriah looks around. Nothing seems to be out of place, and she can't see any spirit intruders. Humbly she accepts Illumina's words.

"Thank you. I am relieved that the Lord sent you to tell me that."

Illumina fades away.

Moriah prays. "Lord, use me and make me or break me. I'm yours. I will fight your fight to save that which is lost."

Again, Moriah notices a presence behind her. She takes a deep breath. With her head half turned, but not looking behind her, she commands. "Get away from me you unclean brood, in the Lord's name."

Moriah sees a couple of ugly unclean spirits scramble and PUFF they all disappear involuntarily.

Moriah smiles and goes on her way with a few skips.

*

It is Tuesday. Vincent gives a tour for a group of people through the hallway of his school. Moriah pushes Mr. Hanes' wheelchair, and Diane walks beside them.

They look through a large window and watch a Kickboxing class. Two students with boxing

gloves and bare feet and shorts are kicking
each other.

Vincent explains. "This is Thai boxing.
Students may use the hands with the boxing
gloves and the legs and feet. It is the
national sport of Thailand.

Diane is amazed. "So, did you go to
Thailand too?"

Vincent nods. "Yes, Diane. Thailand is
exquisite."

The one student kicks the other one right
in the ribs.

Diane reacts. "Did you see that guy
kicking the other one? That must have hurt."

Moriah shrugs her shoulders. "But they
know that if they fight it will hurt
eventually."

Diane relaxes. "Sure they know, the
exciting part is the learning, then you can
block the blows."

Moriah shakes her head. "Why would anyone
want to fight knowing that they get hurt? I
don't like violence."

The group continues the tour. They stop at
the next window. Six students train dressed in
their white Tae Kwon Do suits. David is one of

them. They are in a line, hands balled into fists, arms on guard. They sidestep.

The Trainer gives directions. "Front kick, step left, right, sidekick. Down, step right, left, sidekick…"

Diane is impressed. "Wow. That's a good workout. And David looks like he's been doing that for a long time."

Mr. Hanes sounds like a proud father. "David is an excellent fellow. Vincent, what about that strong fist? Are there any Thai Chi classes going on right now?"

Vincent points to the next window. "Yes, right in here. And two more classes, one for Karate and the other for Kung Fu."

Moriah follows Vincent and wheels Mr. Hanes to the Thai Chi window. The room has a wall-to-wall mirror.

Like a boy receiving a present, Mr. Hanes watches eagerly through the window. His hands curve. He makes the same movements with his upper body, arms, and hands like the students. He flexes his arm muscles in slow motion.

Moriah lets Mr. Hanes be and moves forward following the group ahead watching the rest of the training classes. "Mr. Hanes, I'll check the other classes out… Diane, wait for me."

Moriah runs toward the group. Diane looks through a window and waves Moriah to her.

Inside is a Karate class performing blocking with forearms. Some pairs have fists and others train with open hands.

The next window has Kung Fu with students in black uniforms practicing a close-range-fighting technique with hands and arms ('sticking hands.')

Diane steps back. "I think I like David's class best. Maybe I'll join for a while."

Moriah encourages Diane. "I'm sure it's good exercise. I'll pass. I just don't see reason on the fighting part."

Diane tries to explain. "Tae Kwon Do is self-defense. Maybe one day you might be able to defend someone other than yourself if you'd learn and train."

Moriah shrugs one shoulder. "It's still fighting. I'd rather find a more peaceful way to help."

Diane puts her arm around Moriah's shoulders. "I know you would. But you never know what's going to happen. There's a lot of wrong in this world."

Moriah is surprised hearing Diane say these words. "Hm… Well, I hope you have fun. I just don't feel like doing it right now."

The two have reached the end of the hallway. A glass case with photos hangs on the wall right next to a closed wooden door. Diane tries to get inside. "I wonder what's in here. Maybe a bathroom?"

Vincent catches up with them. He flashes an embarrassed smile. "This is closed. Don't open it."

He steps right in front of the door that the girls can't get inside.

Diane wants to know. "Why? What's in this room?"

Vincent blows air out of his mouth. "If I wanted to show it to you, I would have. Just go back to the classrooms."

Moriah is all right with that and starts to walk back down the hallway. But Diane is stubborn and stays put, especially because Vincent told her not to open the door. She puts her hands on her hips. "You haven't changed a bit since High School. Full of secrets. I bet there's nothing behind that door."

She turns in a flash and opens the door. She looks inside from the place she stands.

Vincent answers a bit rash. "And you haven't changed with your nosiness. I wish you wouldn't do that."

The room is open. It is small and has a sink, a mattress, neatly folded blankets, an exercise floor mat, a folded stack of clothing, a pair of street shoes, some books; all in all some very simple items.

Vincent sighs. "That's where I sleep. It's just a small room with a bed and a sink."

Moriah stops in her tracks, turns and walks back to Diane and Vincent. She looks inside. "Is that all the stuff you own?"

Vincent smiles sheepishly. "What you see is all I have. I don't want to clutter my life with things.

Diane is a bit disappointed. "No TV, no computer? I didn't know, Vincent."

Now, Vincent grins. "There's life even without a computer or TV. I like being here and I have my money invested in this school."

As Diane thinks about it more, she is impressed. "Actually, that's kind of cool."

Vincent steers both of them back away from his room door.

Diane thinks about the situation. "Your school is a pretty big place. And you have lots of showers in the locker room. But what do you eat?

Vincent laughs. "Food of course… I have all I need. Thanks. Did you like the tour?"

The three return down the hallway to the classes.

Diane says dreamily, "We loved the tour. I would like to join David's class."

Moriah points to Mr. Hanes. "Look at Mr. Hanes over there. He found his favorite."

Vincent smiles and says. "Schedules hang up on the wall by the entrance. Find a beginner's class and show up early for your uniform and things."

Vincent stops and gets the girl's attention to another glass case hanging on the wall. It has different uniform patches.

"Oh, and look at these patches, after you earned your blue belt you'll get one."

Diane is very interested. One of the patches shows a tiger, another a leopard, a dragon, a crane, a snake and an eagle.

Diane calls out, "Beautiful."

Vincent continues. "They each have a meaning. Which one do you like best?"

Moriah and Diane look at the patches closer.

Diane chooses the crane. "I like the crane. It is magnificent."

Vincent smiles. "The Crane stands for grace and balance. And you, Moriah?"

"I like the eagle best."

Vincent is surprised. "That's funny. It isn't a school patch. I like it because it reminds me of the Scripture: Those who wait on the Lord shall renew their strength, and they shall mount up with wings as eagles."

"Cool." Says Moriah, "I like that scripture too. I'm glad you still remember some of the Bible even though you've been gone so long and all."

Vincent laughs. "You're funny."

They walk toward Mr. Hanes. He is happy to see them. He points with glee through the window, at a pompous woman.

"Guys, look at that. Alberta Gong and her friend Doris Dimm are in this group. That means double the fun, exercise and knowing about the latest gossip in town."

Moriah and Diane look searching through the window.

Alberta Gong, an about 49-year-old overweight woman with a red face, is paired up with her younger friend Doris Dim, in her early 40s. She is a skinny tall white-faced woman. They look like an odd couple together.

Moriah gets it. "Now that is… Hm… Right up your alley?"

Diane bursts out. "Spectacular and funny. Yeah, go for it, Mr. Hanes."

They break out in laughter.

*

Moriah loves to jog early in the mornings when hardly anyone is out on the streets. She inhales the fresh air deeply. The horizon is set ablaze with the promise of dawn. Fog covers the meadow.

Moriah turns her headset on. She listens to P.O.D. 'Alive… I thank God for every breath

I take…' She jogs. Her jogging suit has reflector bands about two inches wide around both arms and right below both knees and on the outside of her arms and legs, like an outline.

After a good run, she stops at her favorite bench. She is out of breath and sits down. She takes the headphones off of her ears and looks at the sunrise.

She takes a drink out of her small water bottle.

Anger pops out of thin air and stands behind Moriah. With his fingers, he feels around the back of her head looking for an entrance.

Moriah prays out loud. "All I think about day and night is Bella and how to help her. Her dad just makes me so angry, and I can't shake it off. Lord, where are YOU? Are you listening?—"

A YELP escapes from the grass along the path. Moriah gets up and walks toward it. She sees a small dog lying like dead on the lawn. She speaks softly to him. "Hey, little fellow. It's okay. What's wrong? Let me see."

Moriah bends down to give it a closer look. The dog is bloody and dirty. He winces when Moriah touches him.

"Ouch, sorry. I don't want to hurt you, only help."

She turns the collar to find out who the owner is. The collar has a name and telephone number. "Smith, 555 1212. I can't believe this. You belong to that monster of Bella's dad! I'm not going to bring you back there. But I know just the place where we can get you washed up and fed. Mr. Hanes will love you to health."

Moriah can't believe how horrible Bella's Dad can be. She is shaken up. At this moment Hurt appears and grins at Anger. He shows Anger his index finger to wait a moment. Then Hurt pierces Moriah's heart from the back. At the same time, Moriah breaks out in a rush of sobs and tears flow plentifully.

Hurt steps back and makes way for Anger to do his thing. And like on a string, Anger can put his hand inside of Moriah's head and scramble with it. Moriah's presses her lips together in anger, and her tears stop.

Anger and Hurt give each other the 'high fives.' Then they dissipate.

Moriah takes her sweat jacket off and lays it on the ground. She manages with great care to put the dog inside and picks him off the ground. She cradles him and goes back on the path and walks to Mr. Hanes' home.

*

Diane starts her new Tae Kwon Do class. She fusses with her uniform and tries to straighten all folds of her jacket. Other students are in the room, and all are wearing white uniforms with a white belt around their waists and bare feet.

Some of the students are working on stretching exercises.

The door opens, and Diane can't believe her eyes. Moriah walks through the door wearing a brand new uniform. Her hair is tied into a ponytail. She walks right up to Diane with her white belt in her hand.

Hurt and Anger are attached to Moriah's back of her head. She doesn't smile as usual.

Diane is excited. She blurts out, "Wow. You came! What made you change your mind?—

66

Moriah interrupts. "Lots of things, and what you said about defending someone else someday, you hit the nail on the head. What do you do with the long belt?"

Diane reaches out and grabs Moriah's belt. "Sure… Let me tie it on you. Watch." She folds the belt in half in the middle. Then Diane swings the belt around Moriah's waist and loops the two loose ends into a double knot.

Moriah tells Diane, "Mr. Hanes is in the other room feasting on Alberta Gong's gossipy news."

Diane laughs. "Fun… for him. By the way, I don't really know how to tie a belt. But, you know, the way I wrapped it, it won't open during practice… Here he comes. Isn't he good looking? First warm-ups, later we partner up."

Diane looks at the door, and so does Moriah. The trainer comes into the classroom. "Hello, class. Let's do warm-ups."

He walks over to the sound equipment and turns on some music. Then he claps his hands and motions for the students to line up.

Moriah can't believe her eyes. It is the same young man who had his quarrel with his young wife next door to Mr. Hanes. She whispers to Diane. "I know him. He is Mr. Hanes' neighbor."

Diane glances at herself in the mirror and then fusses with her hair. "I think he looks smashing. What do you say?"

Moriah shakes her head. "I don't like to be the bearer of bad news for you Diane, but he's already taken. He has a cute little wife at home."

Diane looks disappointed. She sighs. "Our town is so small, that there are no good ones available."

Moriah disagrees. "Wait a minute. Just because someone looks good doesn't mean that he or she is good—"

The trainer sees Moriah and speaks up to the class. "Oh! We have a new student. I'm glad to see you, again."

He bows slightly. Moriah blushes and gestures a bow back.

The trainer says, "I hope to see you in future classes."

Moriah answers. "Thank you."

Diane is amazed and elbows Moriah. She whispers. "Are you keeping secrets from me?"

Moriah shakes her head and whispers. "No. I told you I'd seen him before when I left Mr. Hanes' house one afternoon."

Diane looks at the trainer with a keen eye. "He would have made a handsome friend."

Moriah answers her back. "There's always room for more friends."

The students line up. The Trainer sits down on the floor. "All right ladies, no more chit chatting! Let's get to work. And touch the toes and stretch."

The students are reaching, imitating every movement the trainer makes. Moriah and Diane scramble to the floor and try to catch up with the action.

As soon as Moriah sits down, Hurt and Anger disappear.

The Trainer lies down on the floor. "Now sit ups... hop, down, hop, down..."

*

Hurt and Anger flee out of the room like something haunts them. Hurt wines, "The next thing she would have done is lie down and discovered us. That was a close encounter."

Anger grumbles, "I was so close to blinding her inner eyes and she wouldn't have seen us. Oh, look over there. Who do we have here?"

Hurt looks the direction Anger is pointing. Warrior-Foe stands there, bored, drumming his fingers on the wall with one hand. "What kind of baby play are you playing? You are ineffective. She doesn't even look mad."

Anger puffs himself up. "What do YOU know? You think you can just show up in our territory and boss us around?"

Warrior-Foe rolls his eyes and pretends to think intensely. Then he attacks the two with his hot temper. "YES. I CAN. And look at that pitiful Hurt. Come over here."

In a theatric gesture, Warrior-Foe swings his arm for Hurt to get closer.

Hurt joins the two with sagging shoulders. "If you'll let me do my job—"

Warrior-Foe interrupts. "Your job is to make her feel sorry for herself, not for someone else. Do you even understand why?"

Hurt looks timid with his big eyes. "I'm trying—"

Anger chimes in. "Trying isn't hard enough. Do it."

Warrior-Foe pushes Anger aside. "Listen you halfwit. You've got your work to do. Hurt, if earthlings feel sorry for themselves they are open for finding suggestions and excuses. And that's when they are open to let Anger in. Do you understand that?" Warrior-Foe waits for a response from Hurt but doesn't get one. "When an earthling feels sorry for someone else, they stay healthy and protected."

Hurt grumbles in his whiny voice. "I can't do anything right for anyone. Can I? And now, he's even telling me how to do my job."

Warrior-Foe is disgusted. "I'm right here. Whatever, just go and work."

Anger and Hurt turn to leave back into the classroom. Warrior-Foe grabs on to them preventing them from sliding through the glass any further.

Anger is surprised. "What the--?"

Warrior-Foe is steaming. "Not from the front of the girl. She will see you."

Anger scratches his head. "Oh… right."

Hurt shies back. "I'll wait my turn."

71

Warrior-Foe turns away from them and strides like a mad bull toward Vincent's closed door. "No wonder there isn't any real damage done here with these earthlings when everyone is monkeying around. I'll show them how it's done."

He reaches the door down the hallway and zips right through it.

*

Vincent sits crossed legged on a flat pillow in the middle of his room. He is meditating facing the wall decorated with an assortment of martial arts weapons and a narrow table with lit candles.

Warrior-Foe assesses the situation. He starts manipulating Vincent's mind. At first, he spreads his cloak around Vincent. Then he holds his hands around Vincent's head without touching him.

Purple light flashes with black lightning from Warrior-Foe's hands penetrating Vincent's mind.

While Warrior-Foe speaks with his suggestive and eerie voice, Vincent experiences a flashback of his past he has tried to run away from. "Remember, when you started your skills and your opponents defeated you? They won and beat you. That hurt not only your body but also on the inside of you."

Vincent cringes by this memory.

Warrior-Foe continues agonizing Vincent. "Remember when you had fallen in love with the prettiest girl in the whole wide world? Then her father gave her hand to a Korean just because you are a Westerner."

Vincent sees his love, a beautiful Korean girl his age, with the eye of his mind. She smiles at him, and he smiles at her. Then her father comes along. He is angry. He pulls her away from him and gives her hand to his opponent Cho Ming. Soon they hold hands getting married and a flower circle surrounds them.

Vincent squirms being plagued by this memory. He sweats with agony and grabs his belly. "Ouch. Arrgh. Oww."

Warrior-Foe enjoys himself. His mean grimace turns meaner still. He lets go of Vincent's head, but circles him carefully, whispering into his ears. "You had worked so hard. You even signed your soul over to 'The

Ancient Secrets of Martial Arts.' Accomplished
one black belt after another…"

Vincent experiences another flashback. He
is fighting with his peers. His Master is proud
of him and gives him one award after another.
He suddenly stands by a coffin.

Warrior-Foe is relentless with his words.
"Your skills got better and better. Then your
Master died. He left you. And then you left,
just like that. The father of your love gave
her to another, and you had nothing left. Take
revenge. Revenge yourself for all the wrong
done to you. Revenge…"

The flower-covered coffin is in front of
Vincent. He stares at a photo of his old Master
with his long white beard and long white hair
and kind eyes. In the memory, Vincent's face
changes to stone, and he pounds his fist on the
coffin.

Vincent tries to shake off the memories.
He shakes his head and holds it with both
hands. He pulls himself up staggering to the
wash basin. He grabs the water pitcher standing
next to the basin. Bending down, he pours water
with the pitcher over his head. He puts the

pitcher down. His hair is dripping wet. Vincent just stands there, bent over and thinking.

Warrior-Foe tries to enter Vincent, but he bounces back. He turns to leave. "Soon you are mine. Then you won't even know what hit you. Hahahaha."

Warrior-Foe vanishes. Vincent breathes deeply. Then he washes his face again and dries it with a towel. He looks at himself in the mirror on the wall.

Knocking on the door brings Vincent out of his stupor. He puts the towel down and combs his hair back with his hands. He takes a few deep breaths and walks to the door and opens it.

Vincent stares at Mr. Hanes in surprise. "Oh, H. come on in. I just washed my hair. I'm a bit wet." He opens the door wide.

Mr. Hanes rolls his wheelchair inside the room. "I hope I'm not interrupting." He sees that Vincent is as pale as a sheet. "Why, Vincent? Are you feeling well?"

Vincent waves off Mr. Hanes' concern. "I'm okay. It's just… never mind."

Mr. Hanes looks around the room and admires the weapons on the wall. "You are here day and night, aren't you?"

Vincent nods.

Mr. Hanes speaks cheerfully. "I have this spare room in my place. I won't mind having company, if you want to get away from here, at least for the nights? I'd be happy if you would stay with me."

He looks at Vincent with a measure of expectation. It takes Vincent a few moments to answer. "That's awfully sweet of you H. I'll think about it, and I have a feeling already, that I might take you up on it."

Mr. Hanes reaches his hand up to Vincent for a handshake. "Good. And I came by to tell you what a grand time I had in your class."

Vincent smiles at Mr. Hanes. "Thanks, H. I'm glad you enjoyed it. Does that mean you're coming back?"

Mr. Hanes wheels his chair around and out of the room. "Ha. You bet I'll be back as often as I can. I feel great."

Vincent stays in his room, and Mr. Hanes wheels down the hallway. He stops at the Tae Kwon Do classroom window.

Inside, the students are partnered up. Two by two they practice defense techniques. Moriah and Diane are partners.

Diane looks at her forearm. "Why are you so rough today? Look at my arms and my shins. They are black and blue."

Moriah looks at Diane's wrists and then her own. "I've got red marks too. Isn't that normal?"

Diane rubs her forearms. "No, not like that. Are you all right?"

Moriah answers quickly. "I'm fine. I'm always fine!"

Diane gets into Moriah's face. "I'm your best friend, Moriah. You don't even sound like yourself."

The girls don't see the trainer come up to them. "This isn't a chat room. Continue practicing, please, Ladies."

Diane blushes and smiles apologetic. The girls position themselves again into attack and defense position. They are doing the legwork.

The trainer gives them an encouraging nod. "Better, and leg punch. Feet much higher."

He turns to assist other students.

Moriah and Diane follow the trainer's instructions.

Diane comes close to Moriah and whispers. "Coffee tomorrow?" Moriah nods and whispers back. "Yes, sounds great."

They continue with their leg punches and arm punches, left, then right, then left.

*

Vincent answers a telephone call in the office. He listens and is amazed. Cho Ming is on the other line. "I challenge you to finish the fight, the one you walked away from me. I do not accept this behavior. We agreed that the winner would get you know what."

Vincent is not happy about Cho Ming's words. "As you remember, I told you that I only fought you to show you that I'm at least as good a fighter as you. But I never fought to win her for a price, and you know it. So, you're challenging me to finish the fight? All right, I accept. See you when you get here."

Vincent hangs up the telephone. He stays sitting and blows air. Then in a flash, he jumps into a fighting position. And BAM, he blows a punch with his arm in the air.

*

The next day, Mr. Hanes sits in his favorite spot and watches the birds through his camera. He takes pictures.

Bella's dog Putzi sleeps rolled up on a pillow by the door. He looks well, clean and healthy. He wakes up and wags his tail.

David is the reason he woke up. David bursts from the inside of the house out to the porch. He holds a stack of photos in his hand. He pets the dog with the other one.

He whispers. "Psst, Mr. Hanes, is it safe to come out? I don't want to chase the birds away. Oh, what a cute little dog you are."

Mr. Hanes waves David to come closer. "Come here. It's okay. Putzi? Yeah, I love this little creature. Oh, you have the printed photos."

David nods and puts the photos on the table. He lays them out like cards. He keeps one in his hand. "This one is the one I like best, Mr. Hanes. How did you get that? The woodpecker on the tree trunk, and the chickadee, the bluebird and the two little sparrows eating seeds. That has got to be a winner."

Mr. Hanes wheels his chair closer and takes the photo in his hand, looks at it and other photos all the while talking. "Yes, I remember that one. I sat here not moving, for what felt like over an hour—"

David interrupts. "That's why the birds felt comfortable and came. Well, I have to tell you, that I went ahead and entered that one with the other two you told me to send to the photo competition."

David selects two more photos from the pile and shows them to Mr. Hanes, who takes them and nods with satisfaction.

"We should keep them separated, until the result of the competition is out. Has Vincent moved in yet?"

"Yes. Vincent doesn't own that much, only a few things. So it was a quick move. He should be here any minute."

Just at that moment, Vincent comes out of the house. "Thank you, H. for letting me stay in your home. The room is very nice."

Mr. Hanes smiles. "I'm glad you like it. Come here, Vincent, look. We entered three photos into a photography contest. We think this one will win. What do you say?"

Vincent looks at the photos. "These are beautiful, H. And the details wow. By the way, some students asked me to have pictures taken of them. If you like, you could be the photographer. It's a paying job. I like this one."

He shows the one photo to David and Mr. Hanes. David agrees. "Yeah, I picked that one too. And the job is a great offer. You do know that Mr. Hanes and I are partners here?"

Vincent grins. "Of course I do. The printouts are excellent. I'll let you know as soon as I have more details on what the parents and students want. Now, I've got to run to a meeting at the school. See you later?"

Vincent leaves in a hurry. Mr. Hanes and David wave at him.

Mr. Hanes grabs David's arm. "David, how about that? A job taking photos and you as my partner printing them. But do you even have time to do that?"

"It sounds good to me. Money pays bills. I always have bills, but having the money for it could be tough."

"David, you're a good sport. Ask a busy person to do something, and it gets done."

*

Later on in the afternoon, David pushes Mr. Hanes' wheelchair down the hall in the martial arts school. They pass two Asian men, who stand post on one of the classroom doors. Their black shirts have the Yin Yang symbol on the chest pocket.

David whispers into Mr. Hanes' ear. "What's going on?"

Mr. Hanes shrugs his shoulder. "You got me—"

One of the men takes a step away from the classroom and stands in the middle of the hallway. He looks at David and Mr. Hanes with crossed arms.

David stops the wheelchair at the window for the same classroom the Asian men were standing guard. David and Mr. Hanes look through the window.

Vincent and Cho Ming are arguing inside. They both seem angry, and they are yelling at each other.

Cho Ming pushes Vincent's chest with both hands and storms out the classroom into the hallway. He almost falls over Mr. Hanes' wheelchair. He bows slightly and speeds on his way. His two guards follow him.

Vincent comes out the door and sees his friends. Both look at him with expectancy. And after a few moments, "You are the first to know that we will have a tournament in town. Let's determine a day as soon as possible."

Mr. Hanes and David look surprised and burst out together, "A tournament?"

Vincent tries to look relaxed. "I know it is sudden. The man you just saw is Cho Ming from Korea. He challenged me, and I have to accept to keep my honor. The whole school is invited to attend."

Mr. Hanes nods his head slightly. "Interesting, anything you want to talk about?"

Vincent shakes his head. "Not really. It's just that my past is catching up with me—."

Mr. Hanes raises his eyebrows. "Oh? Well, in that case, I wouldn't want to miss it."

David joins in. "Me too. Should I make some posters?"

Vincent is all for it. "Good idea."

David wheels Mr. Hanes. "Let's get to work then."

*

Meanwhile, in Hell, Lucifer is furious as usual. He kicks demons and hits rocky walls. Everything shakes. It looks and sounds like an earthquake. The Geysers smoke and sizzle.

Besides all the regular wispy Demon-Cowards, Warrior-Foe is also present. He waits for Lucifer to settle down. But Lucifer is far from calming down. He throws his arms up. "Do you see this? It's everywhere."

The creatures around him look baffled. No one knows what Lucifer is talking about.

But he is pointing at the crumbling walls. "My place is under attack because of all the goody two shoes up there, and they are stronger than the whole bunch of you."

Warrior-Foe rolls his eyes and replies in his calm and arrogant way. "If your servants would work the way they should, it all would be a done deal by now."

Lucifer shakes his head. "What are you suggesting? Rage is pretty intense, and the others tell me, it is YOU who is slowing everything down."

Warrior-Foe glances at Lucifer. "Bah, that figures. Always pointing fingers at someone else."

Lucifer is curious. "And what exactly ARE you doing?"

Warrior-Foe is displeased by the turn of the meeting. He never liked Lucifer. "More than you anyway."

Within a split second Lucifer moves from where he stands to right in front of Warrior-Foe. But Warrior-Foe doesn't even twitch. They face each other in a close-up, eye-to-eye.

Lucifer hollers. "Is that so? I could show you how it is done right now."

Warrior-Foe stares at him, boiling on the inside, but calm on the outside. "If you wish. Except, up there we are not allowed to do anything unless an earthling opens up to us. If we don't abide by the rules, it will create a major problem with the Bright side. And You know it."

Lucifer turns away in disgust. He walks to his throne and slumps down on it. "You didn't have to bring that up. Did you? It's not like I forget about it. EVER!"

The rumbling and shaking in hell increase. Lucifer is fuming mad. Warrior-Foe continues pestering Lucifer. "I will follow my plan and finish it successfully. Not like YOU, when you failed to put your throne higher than the Almighty's throne. All you did then was falling… falling… fall—"

Lucifer spews fire at Warrior-Foe. But before the flames reach their target, Warrior-Foe smirks hatefully at Lucifer and vanishes in an instant.

*

It is a beautiful sunny day not a cloud in the sky. There is hardly any traffic on the roads.

Moriah and Diane sit at a table of the Sidewalk café and eat their ice cream quietly.

Diane ogles sideways at Moriah now and then but continues enjoying her ice cream.

Moriah sighs and leans back in her chair. "All right, what is it that you want to know?"

Diane is relieved that the silence is broken. "Well, something is bothering you. It's making you grumpy, and I just don't get it why you are not telling me about it. We always tell each other everything."

Moriah takes a few moments before she answers. "Well, there're a lot of things going on in my life right now. One important thing confuses me so much that I don't know what to do or say." She looks at Diane who licks her ice cream.

Moriah surveys the area around them. Seeing nothing unusual, she lowers her head and whispers. "An angel told me the other day, not to talk about certain things. So many weird things are happening around me, and I wouldn't even begin to know what's going on. And coming to think of it, I probably shouldn't even talk about that I don't know anything."

Diane shrugs her shoulders. She leans closer to Moriah and whispers. "Why aren't you allowed to talk about it?"

Moriah considers how to answer her friend. Then she speaks in a whisper, "I think the best example is: when an army has a battle plan, they don't tell the enemy what they are going to do, or they would be defeated."

Diane is at a loss. Her hushed voice has an edge to it. "What has that to do with you not telling me anything? I'm not your enemy."

A shady looking man in his twenties staggers toward the table next to the girls. He wears a hoody with food and stains all over him. He looks like he just climbed out of a dumpster.

The girls stop whispering immediately and watch the person. Diane covers her nose with the back of her hand. She is sensitive to bad smells.

The shady looking man gives them a loathsome stare. After what seems to be minutes, he huffs at them. "What?"

Diane shies back and looks away.

Moriah asks him with all sincerity. "Can I buy you a sandwich?"

The man shoots from his chair and leaps toward the girls. When he shouts, he spits. "Why would I want you to buy me a sandwich, baby doll? Do I look like I need food? How about a twenty? Can you give me that?"

Moriah shakes her head. "No, I don't want to give you money, food, yes, but no money."

Diane, still holding her hand in front of her nose, anticipates what's happening next.

A waitress and most customers are staring at the man, and he realizes that people are watching him.

The shady looking man steps backward toward his table. He doesn't look, and when he wants to sit down, he almost misses his chair but gets a hold of the table and maneuvers noisily to sit down. He continues keeping his eyes on the girls with hostility.

Diane takes the menu card and fans the smell away.

Moriah whispers again. "I think I see something. Watch this." She puts her elbows on the table and cups her hand in front of her mouth and looks at the man, so it seems. "You unclean spirit, I tell you in Jesus' name to get out of this man. Right now!"

The man's hostile gaze changes immediately into a softer appearance. He looks at his hands, then at his clothes. He takes a napkin and wipes some of the food off his clothes. He sees Moriah and walks over to her. He seems shy and asks hesitantly, "Say, lady, did you just offer me a sandwich?"

Moriah smiles at him. "Yes, I did. Would you like a bacon lettuce and tomato sandwich?"

The man nods.

The waitress is nearby.

Moriah waves her over. "Please, give this man a bacon lettuce and tomato sandwich, and a large bag of chips, and a pint of milk. I'll pay for it."

By now the man is in tears of joy and thankfulness. "Thank you. Bless you." He follows the waitress.

Diane is baffled. "What just happened?"

Moriah shrugs her shoulder. "This man was bound by an unclean spirit and ended up here to bug us. I don't know. I'm glad that he's free now."

Diane agrees almost aggressively. "Me too! Hopefully, he'll get a bath soon and clean clothes."

Moriah laughs, "That's details, Diane. Those kind of things don't matter, the outside dirt and stuff. We should worry about the inside of a person. Oh, my ice cream is soft, just the way I like it." She licks her cone fast.

After a while, Moriah puts her hand on Diane's arm. She speaks again in a hushed voice. "Back to the talking subject, the bottom line is, when we talk, do you know the enemy is also listening? As a matter of fact, the whole universe can hear what we are saying. Now is that creepy or what?"

Diane listens with her mouth open; she seems to understand. "It makes sense. I never knew that."

Moriah keeps on chattering. "Proof is when I whispered into my hand for this unclean spirit to leave this man alone, the man couldn't hear me because I was whispering. But that unclean spirit heard me just fine."

Diane's eyes widen in amazement. "That's right; that's the way it happened."

Moriah hesitates. She pulls out a small notebook and opens it. "Mr. Hanes suggested, writing down the strange things, and the spirits I'd encounter. And he's right. It somewhat keeps things in perspective."

She moves her index finger along the lines on the pages. "Here, I made notes of the events and also who is involved. I'm hoping that somehow everything comes together and the picture will be clear on what the assignment is."

Diane agrees. "That's an excellent idea."

Moriah looks into the notebook and reads. "Anger, Strife, Rage are mainly involved. They are somewhat cousins, if I may say that. And the places and people: Well, it started when I saw them quarreling in an alley. The next day, a young couple fought, and they were mad at each other, that's Strife and perhaps Anger. Bella's dad at the hospital, that could have been rage? I'm not sure, and that's all I have for now."

Diane thinks about this for a moment. "Those demons all have a bad temper and are fighting demons, in a way, and now you are in the Martial Arts School. God knows, there might be a real significant plot connection from the dark side. Maybe they want to pollute a lot of people that they'd end up in hell? Or maybe just one person?"

Moriah nods. "That's what I thought too because the Trainer is the man from the couple. And I believe that the Lord wants to protect them all. I wish I'd know more. I learn as I go. It's frustrating."

Diane licks the last of her ice cream with intensity. "I'm sure the Lord can let you know at the right time."

Moriah sighs. "That's another thing, I didn't think it would affect me at all, but now, I feel like my prayers go nowhere. And if I feel that way, I'm also asking myself, am I the right person for this?"

Diane pats Moriah's hand. "The confusion and your feelings could be because you are angry at the Dad. We are supposed to love the people."

Moriah seems defeated. "I know you're right, but no matter what I do, I can't find anything nice to think about him. So I feel like I'm staying mad with him all the time."

Diane looks worried and says, "You know we all get mad sometimes, but there's a difference of being mad here and there and staying mad and not being able to shake it off."

Moriah frowns and answers sharply. "I know that, Diane, I don't need a lecture from you."

Diane is taken back by the harsh words, but stays quiet.

A convertible car crawls along the road and passes the girls in first gear. A woman with a big hat looks straight at Moriah and yells waving her arms and shaking her fists. At one point she even tries to stand up behind the wheel and lean out of the car.

The woman screams at the top of her voice. "You trouble maker. Do everyone a favor and move out of this town. Who needs someone like you, messing up people's lifes."

The car passes, but the woman still yells out loud.

Diane asks Moriah. "Who is that? Someone else you made mad?"

Moriah shakes her head. "I have no idea. I've never seen her before."

Diane is surprised. "Really? Now that's funny."

The two get into a laughing fit. Moriah speaks out loud the words she writes into her notebook: "If you are talking about the Lord's business, all kinds of things can happen from

94

the dark side. Remember the Sidewalk Café, the unclean spirit in the man and the lady in the car screaming like crazy at Diane and me."

*

It is a quiet night, especially in Mr. Hanes' house. Everyone is asleep. Vincent sleeps soundly in his new room. It's been a long time since he slept in a real bed with sheets and fluffy pillows.

The light from the streets sheds a dim light inside. An Angel of light sits in a corner. However, his light looks like it is on its last power. He is more like gray colored and not happy at all. But suddenly he rises, and there is a flicker coming from him. He knows who is coming before he can see him.

Warrior-Foe appears. He assesses the room and sees the Angel of light, Vincent's Guardian Angel. He takes a step toward him. The Guardian Angel puts his hand to his sword.

Warrior-Foe belittles his opponent. "Bah! I am still his master because he wants it that way. And just look at you. You don't have any power because he doesn't want you. That is pretty funny. Hahahaha."

The guardian's light beams radiantly and uncovers his gleaming sword without touching it.

Warrior-Foe covers his eyes and turns away from the brightness.

Guardian says, "I am always able to defend myself if I must."

Warrior-Foe shields himself with his cloak. "I am not here for you. Stay out of my business."

Guardian's light stays bright. "You think he is your business? You will not succeed. You'll see. He has the living Word of the Lord in his heart. It shall rise to the surface in due time."

Warrior-Foe tries to step between the Angel and Vincent. His cloak shades his eyes, helping him to do that. "Get out of my way."

The Angel of Light steps back into the corner. "The Lord on High sits in the heavens and laughs."

Warrior-Foe turns away from the light. He tries to ignore the Angel. "Is that so? Watch me."

Warrior-Foe changes his appearance into Vincent's Master of Dans. He looks just like the white haired and bearded Master he buried in Korea. Only now he carries this aura looking like an ancient Asian man, full of wisdom. His eyebrows have long hair, and his cheekbones are high.

He wears a black uniform and in his arms is a cat without a head. He touches sleeping Vincent on his forehead. He speaks with an eerie voice. "You are mine. You swore yourself to me. Do not break your vows. The oath you swore is an ancient covenant. Because of it, you are what you are now. Do not break it, or you will end up like this creature in my arm."

Vincent wakes up and sees the Master of Dans and the headless cat. He scrambles trying to sit up. "Master!"

Warrior-Foe continues in the Master's voice. "Do not break your oath. Choose to live and fight. Revenge yourself…"

Vincent is horrified. "Noooo."

The Master disappears. Vincent remains in bed. Beads of sweat cover his face and chest.

The Angel of light draws closer to Vincent and whispers in his ears. Vincent doesn't see him, but the words are soothing. "It was just a dream. It isn't real. Vincent, turn back to the Lord. Give your life to him."

A handkerchief is at the bedside. Vincent grabs it and wipes his face and neck dry. Then he lies back down to find more sleep.

*

At the same time, Moriah is out running in the Park. Besides her, the Park is vacated. The reflector bands of her sweats blink now and then. She listens to music. She slows down and stops.

She turns her music off and takes the headset off of her ears. She listens. All is quiet. She turns and looks around to see if someone follows her. She feels uneasy but continues jogging without the music.

Fear is behind her. He reaches his finger to the back of her neck trying to creep deeper. Every time he does, Moriah turns around to see if someone is after her.

Moriah whispers to herself. "This is ridiculous. I'm not afraid, usually… here we go: In the Lord's name, Fear, I bind your power. Get away from me."

These words blast Fear away from Moriah. Fear can't stop himself from zooming farther and farther away. He is powerless, and his frustration doesn't help at all. Soon he is out of sight.

Moriah is amazed, even though she didn't see Fear fly away, she notices the difference. "Isn't that peculiar? That uneasy feeling then was a spirit and the prayer took care of it."

Moriah reaches her favorite bench and sits down. She looks to the darkening sky and inhales the fresh air deeply.

Branches crackle behind her. Moriah is alerted, but she stays sitting on the bench. The branches break right next to her. Suddenly Gene leaps out from the shadow of the trees and bushes.

Moriah shoots up from the bench and faces him.

Illumina, Moriah's Guardian angel appears like a bright light. His wings seem like a whisper. He is huge and observes the situation calmly. Moriah knows he is here, which boosts her confidence, that no matter what, she'll be all right.

She keeps her eyes focused on Gene, just in case he's planning something unpredictable. She takes a deep breath and positions herself in self-defense.

Gene sneers. "Here we are, just the two of us. No one else is around. I wonder if you are that brave now like you were when you talked to my wife."

Moriah shakes her head. "You couldn't talk to me a few days ago? You had to hide and wait for a moment like this, to bully someone around?"

Anger taps into Moriah's head from behind and tries to take over. "Look at him, this coward and wife beater. How can anyone like him? He hurt his little girl and her cute doggie."

Moriah fights back these intruding thoughts. She also attempts to keep space between herself and Gene.

Gene looks like he is going to lash out at Moriah.

Illumina attempts to pull Anger away from Moriah. Anger flashes his angry look at

Guardian. "She lets me, see. You have no power right now, and never will again. She is a goner from the bright-side and gone to the Darks. Hahaha. See, she doesn't even see me anymore. I could dance in front of her, and she wouldn't notice." Anger does just that. He swoops in front of Moriah and dances a two-step.

Illumina lets go of Anger, but he doesn't leave Moriah's side.

Moriah stays focused on Gene. Her gift is ineffective when she gives in to her human feelings instead of listening to the Lord's voice. All she knows right now is, that Gene hurts people, and she doesn't like him.

Moriah talks roughly to Gene. "You think you're strong? Let me tell you what I believe you are, a coward, waiting—"

Gene is very close now. He interrupts Moriah. "I don't want to know what you think. You've done enough thinking and talking. Stay away from my wife and child. You are telling them lies about me and turning them against me."

Moriah furs her brows. "What?"

Gene tries to grab Moriah by her shoulder. Moriah blocks his hand smoothly. He tries to

get her with his other hand and she blocks it
with her lower arm. Gene is fast and moves
swiftly behind Moriah and grabs her from the
back around her upper chest and neck.

Moriah has enough time to throw her arms
to the front of her chest. She tries to free
herself, but his grip is iron tight.

Gene sneers. "You still think I'm not
strong? I'll show you."

Moriah takes a deep breath and with both
of her arms she pops his grip open. She turns
at the same time and trips him that he falls to
the ground on his back.

Anger has a heyday of a time and hops back
and forth from Moriah to Gene, and all the
while yodeling.

Moriah is influenced by Anger but doesn't
know it. In a split second, Moriah jumps on
Gene. Her knees hold his arms down. She has her
right arm and fist flexed and looks ready to
strike Gene powerfully.

Gene only laughs. "Yes, go ahead, do it.
Give me a good reason to report YOU to the
police and tell them, that it was you, who hit
my daughter and my wife. And now me. Hahaha,
that's a good one." He laughs hysterically.

Illumina puts his hands on Moriah's shoulder. Moriah's jaws tighten. She opens her fist and releases Gene. She gets up and stands there looking at him. "Or, you could just beat me up, like you usually beat up your wife, and I could report you. Make everyone's day!"

Anger is attached to Moriah and enjoys himself. He sees Rage approaching. "Rage! It's about time that you join me. I've been wrestling with them all by myself. Where have you been? Together we could have finished them already."

Illumina crosses his arms and watches the show before him.

Rage doesn't answer but gets busy with Gene's thoughts. Gene balls his fists. His facial expression turns mean. "I just wanted to tell you to stay away from my wife and daughter, or else. Here is my warning, if you don't leave them alone, it won't be a beating, more like a silencing for good."

All Moriah can do is stare at Gene in unbelief how wicked he is. She is so mad at him, and can't shake it off. It takes a lot out of her not to lose control.

Anger whispers to Moriah. "Just punch him out once and for all. Then he'll leave his wife and little girl alone."

Rage whispers into Gene's ear. "We'll get even with her. Very soon. Just don't get caught."

Moriah is torn to either hurt Gene or to let him go. She balls her fists again, but thinks twice about it and turns the opposite direction. "Big shot—"

Moriah takes off jogging.

Gene punches his fists in the air. He is fuming. When Moriah is a distance away, he disappears back into the bushes.

Anger floats after Moriah. "This is my final moment." He zooms in a flash half way into Moriah and right away he puts fog around Moriah's head. Thus he blinds and deafens her to the spirit realm. "Finally, I've got you, and I can talk as much as I want, and you can't hear or see me. Nana nana boo-boo…" He makes raspberries at Illumina and Moriah.

Moriah jogs on. Her face is emotionless and stonelike.

*

One fine sunny Sunday, the weather couldn't be any more gorgeous, the church has their service outdoors. The people sit on the church lawn and folding chairs.

On the side is a large table filled with picnic supplies and lots of food and desserts.

In front is a guitar player finishing up the song "How Great Thou Art."

The people sing heartily. "How great thou art, how great thou art."

The Smith family is there. Gene sings loudly. Rosina sits in the middle and Bella at the end. Bella looks good. She is all healed up now, at least on the outside. Rosina and Bella don't sing. They seem to sit on these chairs like statues.

Diane sings behind them. Her chair is directly behind Bella. David and Vincent sit next to Diane and enjoy singing.

Diane bends forward. She pretends to look for something on the ground and taps Bella slightly on the shoulder.

Bella looks at her dad, who looks toward the guitar player. Bella turns around slowly and sees Diane.

Diane gives her a piece of paper and whispers. "Bella, Moriah found your dog. He is fine and at Mr. Hanes. Here is my phone number."

Bella's face brightens, and she smiles. Her dad turns to see what's going on. He frowns when he sees Bella leaning her head back to Diane. Bella slumps back into her seat, face forward and serious. With great care, that her dad doesn't notice, she puts the piece of paper into her pocket.

Gene looks frosty at Diane, but she resists his cold eyes with spite. Gene suddenly remembers where he is and smiles innocently looking around if anyone watches him. Then he continues to sing with his false smile.

Pride, another dark spirit, dressed in Ludwig XIV clothing because this is, after all, a church, walks arrogantly among the assembled people. His long-haired multicolored wig sparkles in the sunlight. He walks around like he owns everyone.

The song is over, and everyone looks attentively at Pastor Jim Sloan, a somber 35-year-old clerk. He closes the service with prayer. "The Lord bless you and keep you. Please enjoy the food. There's plenty."

The people get up. Many voices rise. A lot of people are talking all at once.

Alberta Gong bullies herself through the crowd toward the Smith's family. Her friend Doris Dim follows her closely. Her long nose looks longer today, because of her thin face.

Both make their way through the crowd with self-importance.

Gene sees them coming and tries to escape. Too late. Alberta calls out. "Oh, Mr. Smith, Mr. Smith."

Gene has no other choice but to stop and look at her and Doris. Alberta keeps on talking. "It is so good to see you. We heard about your daughter's accident."

Gene answers with a slight sarcasm. "I'm sure you have."

Doris Dim nods assertively. Rosina forces a smile. Bella looks to the ground.

Alberta gets right into Gene's face that he has to take a step back. "I can just imagine the worry you must have had. You are a good Dad."

Gene nods. "Thank you for your kind words, ladies. But we have to leave. Bella hasn't fully recovered yet. She tires quickly."

Doris Dim pats Bella on the shoulder. Bella flinches slightly without anyone noticing; except her dad, he sees it right away.

Doris chimes in. "We understand." She bends down to Bella and pinches her cheek. "Little darling get well. Goodbye."

Alberta pulls Doris's arm. She aims toward the food table. "Let's pack a plate, Doris."

Gene grabs their lawn chairs and leads his wife and child to the parked cars.

The pastor sees them trying to leave. He waves and approaches the family. He offers his hand to Gene. "Gene, I'm glad you could join the service today. If I can help you in any way, please let me know.

Gene shakes the Pastor's hand. "Thank you, Pastor. Goodbye."

The Pastor kindly says. "Goodbye, and God bless you."

The Smiths walk a step faster now, away and to the parking lot.

*

The Smiths arrive at their home. They walk
into the entrance. Gene closes the front door.
He pushes his wife so hard that she drops her
purse and gloves. A few items, including a cell
phone, spill out of the bag.

Rosina and Bella are shocked and scared
because they don't know what happened just now.
Bella clings to her mother.

Gene roars. "You are so pitiful, and you
looked pathetic at church. Don't you know that
everyone in the church thinks now something is
wrong with me, because of your behavior?"

Rosina pleads. "We didn't do anything
wrong."

Gene pushes her again. Bella has to let go
of her. Rosina stumbles into the living room,
and he follows her.

Gene hollers. "How about EVERYTHING. You
did everything wrong."

Bella stands shaking in the foyer. She
hears her dad yell at her mom. She looks to the
floor and sees her mother's purse. The cell
phone lies on the floor. Bella checks the
living room door. No one can see her. With

determination and shaking hands, she grabs the cell phone and opens it. She punches 911 and pushes the cell phone back into the bag and grabs the gloves and lays them loosely over the opening of the purse.

Bella freezes when her dad's back appears in the living room doorway. With all her strength for a seven-year-old in danger, she kicks the bag closer to the living room. The bag slides gently along the wall and comes to a halt by the door.

At this moment she can hear the voice, "Hello, what is your emergency?—"

Bella jumps and runs to the living room. She stops at the door and screams louder than the voice coming from the cell phone. "Daddy, Daddy, please don't hurt Mommy."

Her dad wheels around and drones. "Be quiet you little thing."

At this point, Rage appears and hoists on Gene's back and rides him with glee looking like a Rodeo rider on a horse, with only half of the body on top and the lower half inside Gene.

Rosina runs away from Gene. She tries to put the dining room chairs in Gene's way. But nothing stops him. He attempts to run a curve and holds himself on the tablecloth, but it slides down and the vase tips over.

Rosina scoots by a bookshelf. But Gene rocks the whole shelf, and the books fall and spill on the floor.

Rosina is cornered. Fear is gripping her heart and head with his hands and feet like in a vise grip.

Bella runs to Rosina. Rosina's instinct to protect Bella helps her to gain a bit of strength over Fear. And Fear bounces off. Bella and Rosina cling to each other.

Bella pleads. "Daddy, please stop."

Gene pushes a chair out of his path. "Since when do children tell their parents what to do?" He leaps toward both of them. Mother and daughter stand with eyes closed expecting the worst.

Suddenly sirens approach outside, and they seem to stop at their house. Fists are pounding on the front door.

Gene stops cold in his action.

Rage is disappointed and leaves.

Gene comes to his senses and looks around. The living room is a mess. He slumps into a chair, and in a daze, he stares into space.

The pounding outside the house door doesn't stop. "Please, open the door. Open up, or we will come in by force."

Rosina and Bella scoot sideways along the walls out of the living room. They reach the hallway.

Rosina opens the door and gets out of the way.

Two male police officers burst inside with weapons drawn. A quick look around, they see the Dad and handcuff him.

Gene doesn't resist and comes with them. They walk to the door. He looks at Rosina and Bella with sadness. His lips form "I'm sorry." But no tone comes out of him.

Before the officer can lead Gene outside, Bella runs to her dad and hugs him around his belly.

The female officer closes the entry door from the inside. She stays with Rosina and Bella. "Are you all right, Ma'am? Should we call an Ambulance?"

Rosina shakes her head. "No, we are all right. Bella? You?"

Rosina straightens out her hair.

Bella nods. "Okay, Mommy."

The female officer pulls out a notepad. "We have to take in your husband. First, we must find out what happened. After that, we might be able to find help for him. Could we sit down together and talk about this?"

Rosina nods and walks toward the living room. Bella follows. She sees the purse with the cellphone on the floor and picks it up. She takes the open phone out.

Rosina asks the officer. "How did you know?-"

The female officer sees Bella handle the cell phone. She reaches her hand out, and Bella gives her the cell phone. She talks into it. "Hello?"

The operator is still at the other end. "Lisa? Is that you?" "Yeah, it's me. The situation is under control. Thanks, gal."

She closes the phone and gives it to Rosina.

Rosina takes it and asks Bella. "Bella, did you…?"

Bella nods bashfully. Her fingers hold onto her prayer blaze pendant.

The officer smiles at Bella. "Clever trick, Bella. Pretty smart and brave. And for whatever reason, we were right around the corner when we got the call."

Bella smiles. "That must have been angels helping."

The officer laughs. "I bet you're right."

They are in the living room and start picking up things and chairs to sit down. Rosina gets the table in order, and she places the vase upright.

The female officer puts her notebook on the table and sits down. She pulls out a pen. "Let's start from the beginning."

*

The classes are popular at the Martial Arts School. Every single one is maxed out with students.

The T'ai Chi class is in progress. The students wear dark blue uniforms. Mr. Hanes wears the class shirt and his favorite blue sweat trousers. He sits in his wheelchair alongside the group. He moves his arms and upper body just like everyone else.

Alberta Gong is by his side. Doris Dim is on the other side of Alberta.

A female trainer moves in front of the group. Everyone moves with her in unison. "Lift your right knee up slowly and turn the body to the side, plant right foot on the floor and right hand and arm forward into the air."

Mr. Hanes moves his wheelchair into the same direction as the group and moves his arms and hands. He enjoys everything.

Then they repeat the same movements with the left leg, side, foot, hand, and arm. Of course, Mr. Hanes also loves watching the other students moving their legs and feet.

Alberta leans over to Mr. Hanes. She whispers. "I've lost about 300 grams in the last two weeks."

Mr. Hanes raises his eyebrows and pretends to be amazed. "How about that."

Gossip comes along and slobbers from Doris to Alberta. Gossip's saliva does not reach Mr. Hanes. The slobber turns like a boomerang away from Mr. Hanes back to its sender.

Doris Dim whispers and urges Alberta. "Tell him about Smith… Tell him."

Alberta nods in self-importance. "Did you hear about Mr. Smith? He is a wife-beater. He always looked like an angel in the church."

Mr. Hanes widens his eyes. "Who would have guessed that?"

Alberta continues. "And now he is in jail for being a wife beater. He can rot there, for all I care."

The female trainer looks among the students for the whisperers. "Excuse us over there. Please concentrate. Leave worldly troubles away from here. Focus on your innermost being. Move relaxed with mind and body… Flowing… think health."

Mr. Hanes shouts. "And strong fist."

The trainer and the students smile and giggle at Mr. Hanes' balled hands. She says. "Yes, Mr. Hanes. You've got it."

Everyone goes back to concentrating on their T'ai Chi movements.

*

Moriah is taking a shower in the ladies locker room. She lets the water run over her face. It relaxes her.

Diane is already dressed and brushes her hair. "You're taking a long shower today. I'm almost ready to go."

Moriah shouts back. "What did you say?"

Diane speaks louder. "You're taking a long shower today."

Moriah shouts back. "What?"

Diane shakes her head. "Never mind." She tosses her brush inside a bag and walks over to the showers. She takes a bathrobe from the hook next to the shower and opens Moriah's shower curtain and hands her the robe. "Here, you're taking such a long time today. Let's chat."

Moriah turns the water off and grabs the bathrobe and slips into it. She walks to her locker.

Diane sits down on a bench. She is concerned. "Have you seen Vincent today? He looks like he's seen a ghost."

Moriah dries her hair. "No, I haven't seen him. Maybe he's nervous about the tournament?"

Diane shrugs her shoulders. "Yes, Maybe… Are you going to the tournament tomorrow?"

Moriah is getting dressed. She shakes her head. "I'll try to see Bella, and we'll walk Putzi together. And if I get over being mad at her dad, I'd like to visit him in jail, if they let me."

Diane is curious. "Well, are there still strange things happening around you? Maybe your job is Bella's dad?"

"I'm not sure. I wish I would have more info. Usually, the Lord shows me more details, and I could just go forward in His Name and get rid of the unclean spirits. But this time, I don't have the slightest idea. Maybe I'm not on a job at all, and everything was a mere coincidence."

Moriah zips her pants. She swings around and goes into fighting position and launches a punch into the air.

Diane is startled by the fast movement. "You worry me, Moriah. I barely see you smile anymore. Let's pray together and maybe the Lord will show us how to handle all of this."

The blinders flash up around Moriah's head and fade away again. Moriah shakes her head. "Nay, I'm all right. I've prayed. No worries. I like the move we learned today." She punches the air again, right and left. "Pow! Wow!"

Diane shakes her head and gets up to leave. "I'll be praying alone then, and for you. Are you taking Mr. Hanes home?"

"No, Vincent is going to take care of Mr. Hanes. Go ahead. I want to blow dry my hair."

Diane grabs her bag. "See you tomorrow at the tournament.

Moriah nods. "See you then. I might be a few minutes late."

*

The School gym is set up for the competition. There are bleachers all around and additional chairs in the front. There are so many seating areas as if the whole town would be coming to watch the competition.

And truth be told, at least one hundred people are there. All the students are attending. They are sitting together by group discipline. Except Mr. Hanes, Diane and David sit together. Mr. Hanes' wheelchair is in a space by an aisle. Another reserved empty seat waits for Moriah.

119

David asks Mr. Hanes. "Can you see all right?"

Mr. Hanes cranks his neck. "Yes, that's good. And if the people are getting too excited and stand up, I'll just wheel myself to the front."

David nods. "That works."

Over on the other side of the arena, Alberta Gong, and Doris Dim sit together in the front row. They wear colorful headbands.

Alberta is nervous. "If anyone would have told me a year ago, that I would sit here in a tournament and watch a fight, I would not have believed it."

Doris agrees. "I know what you mean. Yeah. But, I feel like- super young."

Alberta bursts the words out. "Me too! With a lot more energy than I've felt in a long time."

Both ladies are beside themselves with the excitement.

At another area are a group of Korean visitors clustering together. They look calm and contained.

The chatter from most of the locals is loud.

The back doors open. The contestants enter through different doors. Vincent wears his white uniform with the golden embroidered eagle in the back and his black belt. Two of his trainers accompany him. They walk along the wall and then through the crowd toward the arena. They pass the students who are in the front row of the bleachers. There are whistling and cheering.

Cho Ming wears his black uniform with the golden and red dragon embroidered on the back and the Yin Yang symbol on the front. Two of his men walk with him along the wall and through the crowd behind Vincent. The people Cheer and Boo. Excitement hangs in the air like static electricity.

Two Referees jump up into the rink. One is from Vincent's group and the other from Cho Ming's team.

Each contestant moves into his corner with his men.

No human sees Warrior-Foe with his gaze fixed on Vincent. His ugly face shows signs of victory. He reaches with his hand to Vincent's head and squeezes.

Vincent looks at Cho Ming with hate-filled eyes.

Cho Ming returns the look.

They approach each other and whisper that no other can hear.

Vincent hisses. "You had to come and challenge me. I spared your life then."

Cho Ming hisses back. "You left with the situation open-ended between us."

Vincent shakes his head. "You stole the love of my life, and you still don't have enough. Are you hoping you'll get proof that you are a better fighter?"

Cho Ming replies, "I know I AM a better fighter. I want the world to know also."

Vincent frowns. "I should have finished you when I had the chance."

They both take a step back and with balled fists, in front of them they bow and wait for the signal to start.

More unseen forces are present. They are an army of small dark demons spread out between bleachers and rows. Their eyes are glowing, and their wings are pulsating and tucked in. These are Warrior-Foe's Minions positioned to influence as many spectators as possible.

Angels of Light are also present. Most of them stand posted along the back of the spectators. And some are closer to the middle. With swords drawn they are ready to fight if anyone would call for help, or if need be.

Guardian Angel protects our group of friends.

Diane is amazed. She points toward the fighters. "Wow, there they are. I've never been in real combat. Isn't that what they call this?"

David nods. "Yeah, except, I found out that it is more like a personal power fight, more like revenge, and THAT worries me."

Mr. Hanes looks up very interested. "Ah, so that's the man who married the girl Vincent had fallen in love with?"

David looks at Mr. Hanes. "Exactly, and somehow they think that they need to work things out with fighting."

Diane looks into the direction of the Korean group. "Where is the girl? Is she here?"

David shakes his head. "She's in Korea and probably doesn't even know that they are fighting for her. It's a guy thing."

He shrugs his shoulder.

The overseer gives the signal to start. A giant gong gets the attention of everyone.

All eyes look toward the rink. The referees give the signal to begin. Music plays some rock fighting tune.

Vincent and Cho Ming bow and circle each other.

Moriah enters the gym and looks for her friends. She spots them and makes her way to them. She sits down next to Diane.

Mr. Hanes is happy to see her. "They just started. You didn't miss anything. It looks like a harmless tackle."

Moriah nods at Mr. Hanes and then looks at the fighters.

Diane squeezes Moriah's arm gently. "Good to see you. Where were you?"

Moriah seems grumpy. "I walked Bella's dog to their house, but no one was home. Then I took Putzi back to Mr. Hanes' house. I am worried. And I just can't shake that nasty feeling toward Gene. He is such a complete jerk."

Diane is concerned. "Maybe you've been working too much. Are you getting enough sleep?"

Moriah shakes her head. "No, I've not worked too much; I haven't been able to get anything done. That whole thing is eating me up on the inside. And I don't like it."

Diane pauses for a few moments. "Can you SEE into the spiritual again? You know?"

Moriah is still grumpy, "No, I haven't seen Angels or Devils in quite some time now. And if you want to know the truth, I don't mind being normal like everyone else."

Diane takes a short breath. "And this isn't worrying you?"

Moriah shrugs one shoulder. "Not at all, why should it?"

Moriah shakes her head and stares at the fight.

Vincent and Cho Ming attack each other fiercely. They attack with hands and block. They kick with the legs and escape. It is an excellent fight.

The crowd loves the entertainment. Alberta and Doris scream their uuhs and aahs.

Diane gets scared and grabs David's arm on one side and Moriah's arm on the other side. "Ouch, it looks like they want to hurt each other."

David blows air. "Nasty stuff. I hope they'll be all right."

Mr. Hanes drones in a calm voice. "Keep the faith. The fight will have an end. I hope it won't be bloody."

Vincent and Cho Ming appear equally strong.

The Music gets louder and faster. The crowd shouts exhilarated, loud and then quiet and holding their breaths, and then loud again.

*

At the same time, Rosina and Bella sit by the telephone, set on speaker phone. They are talking with Gene.

Bella says in her sweet voice, "Dad, I miss you so much. Are you all better now?"

Gene's voice comes from the phone. "I'm still getting better. The people here are trying to help me."

Rosina gets a chance to say something. "Everyone told us not to visit you. But Bella insisted to at least talk with you." She cries.

Bella pats her mother's hand. "Dad, I love you."

Gene answers. "And I love you, Bella, so much. I haven't been a very good father, have I?"

Bella thinks about this for a second. "I don't know, Dad. I do know that you are the only Dad I have. Did you ever ask Jesus into your heart?"

There is this silence from the other end of the telephone. Then Gene asks with surprise in his voice. "What does that have to do with anything?"

Bella explains. "Well, Moriah says, 'Jesus is the only real help for us people, to find our way out of sin or whatever bad it is they have gotten into and can't get away from."

Rosina cries more in silence and wipes her tears and presses her tissue to her mouth that her husband doesn't hear her cry.

There is this long silence. Then Gene admits. "She is probably right. And it sounds very simple Bella, but some grown up things are not always that easy to get rid of."

Bella doesn't give up. "But Dad, have you tried it? Have you asked the Lord into your heart?"

Gene gives in. "Honestly? No. But I do know, Jesus is the son of God, and that he died for our sins." He ponders for a few moments. "That's what I did, or was doing when I hurt you and your mom, SIN. I sinned. Bella, I love you. Can you help me? What should I do or say?"

Bella closes her eyes. Rosina squeezes Bella's hand.

"Dad, say, Lord, please come into my heart and take all the bad things out of me."

Gene recites the prayer after Bella. "Bella, I am so sorry for hurting you. Lord, please come into my heart and take all the bad things out of me, sob, sob, Rosina, Bella, please forgive me. Can you?"

Rosina nods and sobs right into the telephone. "Oh Gene, of course, I forgive you. I love you."

Bella is happy. "Yes Daddy, I've forgiven you already. None of us is perfect. Isn't that what you always say to us?"

Gene chimes from the telephone. "They tell me I have to go now. See you when I'm all better, okay?"

Bella's voice sounds like a bell. "Yes Daddy, goodbye."

Rosina leans closer to the phone. "Bye Gene, get well." She smacks a kiss into the phone.

The other end of the telephone clicks. Rosina pushes the speakerphone button and hangs up.

Bella is excited. She asks, "Please, Mom, I want to tell Moriah that Dad invited the Lord into his heart."

Rosina nods and lifts the receiver. "What's her number?"

Bella shakes her head. "I don't know Moriah's. But Diane gave me hers the other day. Let me get it." She runs into her room and finds the piece of paper Diane gave her at the church picnic.

*

The combat in the competition arena is heated up. The Music seems louder than before and faster.

All eyes are on the fighters. The crowd is mesmerized.

The invisible dark forces, the minions of Warrior-Foe, stir up the people and turn them into a frenzied mob.

The Angels of Light stand there not able to help because the people don't ask for them. They try to get the people's attention, but their focus is on the fight pushing common sense thoughts as far away as possible. They want to see the fight, and they want to see it until the very end no matter the outcome.

Vincent and Cho Ming are hard at it. If one of them falls to the floor, they jump back up again and again.

Warrior-Foe is enjoying the fight. He divides himself into two spiritual bodies; each part influences an opponent. He tells them phrases like, "this is the fight you can End all your pain. You are fighting for your freedom today. Your hands are swords and your feet are swords."

The fighter's faces change into Warrior-Foe's appearance. They fight bitterly. The crowd gets wilder and crazier.

David rubs his eyes. "Is it just me or does it look like twins are fighting?"

Mr. Hanes rubs his chin. "Yeah, it looks that way. I wouldn't recognize Vincent if I didn't know his uniform. What's going on?"

Diane's cell phone sings. At first, she doesn't hear it, but then she pulls it out of her pocket and answers it, never losing sight of the fight. She holds her other ear closed.

"What...? Who...? Moriah?"

She hands the cell phone over to Moriah. Moriah takes it, but she can hardly understand what the other end is saying. "Bella! Are you all right? Wait, please, I can barely hear you, let me get out of this crowd." She jumps out of her seat and hurries up the aisle and out to the Hall.

The music is faint there and so is the crowd. Moriah is the only one in the hall. "Okay, now. Are you all right?"

Bella is excited. "Yes, my mom and I are good. And even better Moriah. My dad asked Jesus into his heart. He cried hard and felt so sorry.

Moriah is somewhat shocked. "Bella you are so brave."

131

Bella continues, "Jesus is going to make him all better now, just as you always tell us."

Moriah becomes quiet. "Yes, he will."

Bella can hardly contain herself. "I wanted you to know first. I've got to go. My mom wants her phone back. Bye Moriah."

Moriah bites her lip and answers. "Thanks Bella for telling me. Bye, now. I'll bring Putzi to your house. But you could pick him up at Mr. Hanes if you like?"

Bella speaks fast. "Oh yes, I'll pick him up as soon as I can and walk him home. He will like that."

"Yes, he will. Goodbye, Bella."

"Bye, Moriah."

Moriah closes the cellphone and slides down the wall to sit on the floor. She grabs her head with both of her hands and supports her elbows on her knees.

Illumina stands next to her and puts his hand on her shoulder.

Anger flees from Moriah but keeps standing beside her, just in case.

Illumina chimes like pipes. "Out of the mouth of babes, Moriah, another lost soul, saved."

Moriah breaks out crying. "Oh God, what have I done? I am sorry for being so angry with everyone and everything. I completely missed what matters."

Illumina speaks firm. "NO. Stop feeling sorry for yourself and know: Your task is still ongoing. Listen. Can you hear them? LISTEN!"

Moriah gasps. She looks at Illumina. Light flows from him to Moriah and gives her strength.

Anger is in pain from the light and shoots out of sight.

Moriah can shake off her fogginess and hears the crowd get louder. She remembers where she is. She jumps off the floor, wipes her tears with her sleeves while she rushes back into the Combat Arena.

Not wanting to see the whole scenery just yet, she keeps her eyes fixed on her path in front of her. She reaches her friends and hands the cell phone back to Diane.

Diane sees that Moriah had cried. "What? Is Bella okay?"

Moriah sits down and nods. Diane points to the fight. "I think I'm going to get sick watching them hurt each other in that violent manner."

Moriah takes a deep breath and looks up to the fight and around the gym. "Oh my God! What? I didn't know!"

She sees that neither Vincent nor Cho Ming is in control of themselves. She recognizes that the demon Warrior-Foe is split up into two forms and each is inside the fighters. She sees the demonic forms handle the men from the inside like puppets. And if the demon forms move arms or legs, the men move in unison.

Warrior-Foe determines that one of the fighters is going to die today then the other one will be his servant.

Moriah is frozen because the fight is so fierce and hateful. Then all at once Lucifer's head appears translucent on the ceiling. He surely is enjoying the whole disaster.

Moriah sees the hordes of minions and demon in control of the crowd. She is abhorred. She looks at Guardian next to Mr. Hanes and friends.

The Guardian knows her unspoken questions and answers them. "The People want that fight. Therefore we are limited to do something about it. Look at the Angels of Light standing around. They wait for someone to call on the Lord. They are not allowed to help unless there is ONE standing in the gap for these people because they don't know what they do. Now you got the essence of your assignment, Moriah."

Moriah sees the Angels of light looking very dim and without power all around the back of the arena. She looks back to the fighters.

Vincent has Cho Ming on the floor and jumps on him. Vincent is struggling not to punch a death blow at Cho Ming. But Warrior-Foe fights from within Vincent's body and seems to succeed.

And in the arena, the demons rule the people. They chant. "Kill him. Kill him."

Alberta and Doris are influenced by this madness, just like everyone else. Their headbands are sideways, and their hair is messy.

Alberta shouts with the people. "Kill him, kill him."

Doris tries to outscream everyone. "Kill him, kill him."

The Music thunders.

Moriah stands up in a flash. She suddenly doesn't hear the shouts anymore. She only hears noises as if she were under water.

Moriah raises her one hand high. She calls out. The spirit world can hear her. They hear every word. Each word stabs and wounds them like a sword.

"Stop, in the name of the Lord! All of you forces of darkness STOP. I bind your power in Jesus' Name."

With these words, it is like time freezes for a few moments. The people scream on, but all the spirit beings may it be dark or light, are stopped and look at Moriah.

The Angels of Light are glad and start to gleam. The demons and minions scramble and push each other. They are whirling around to find out who is disturbing their party.

Moriah prays silently. "Oh Lord, forgive the people, please. You unclean spirits, let God's people go in the Name of the Lord."

The demonic spirits have to let go of the people. The chanting dies down. The people are confused and don't know what's going on.

The Angels of Light recover some of their brilliance and move in to assist the earthlings.

The Minions shade their eyes and turn away from the brightness.

Alberta takes her headband and opens it up to wipe her face and neck. "What just happened?"

Doris shakes her head. "I have no idea. The memory is like a horrible dream and I want to forget it quickly."

Warrior-Foe is forced to stop his power trip over the fighters. He flings out of Vincent and Cho Ming. His split beings shake their heads to assess the situation. They melt again into one body.

All eyes of the underworld, Lucifer, the minions and demons look at Moriah. They are worse than furiously mad. Their voices and wings sound like hundreds of bats flying out of a cave. Moriah can hear some of the voices. "Who is that? How can she do that? Why is she even here? The power belongs to us."

Vincent gains control of himself and gets off Cho Ming.

Both of the men breathe hard sitting on the floor. Their hateful eyes change into an almost apologetic look at each other.

Their helpers and trainers rush to support them helping them off the floor and to the chairs in their assigned corners.

Warrior-Foe's gaze finds Moriah with loathing. He points his finger commanding his minions. "Destroy her."

Moriah panics. She looks at her friends and urges. "Pray for me, for protection." She runs toward the exit.

Guardian Angel stays with her friends and calls after her. "The Lord's Spirit is in you. You know what to do. Remember. Illumina and I are needed here."

All demons follow Moriah.

Vincent's Guardian Angel zooms to Warrior-Foe getting a hold of the back of his neck and punching him into the stomach. He drones, "Give back what you have stolen."

Warrior-Foe chokes and spits out the golden letters he snatched when Vincent requested a pure answer from the Lord. The letters sparkle and rise up freely and disappear.

*

Moriah runs as fast as ever out the door and away from the exit. She wants to protect as many people as possible just in case whatever lies ahead of her will take a while.

She leans up against the building wall.

The swarm of demons is after her, and they cover her like a thick black cloud. They screech. "We are allowed to get you. You opened the door for us. Anger is holding the door open."

Moriah looks terrified at the spirit creatures. Then she closes her eyes and lifts her arms toward the heavens. She breathes deeply. "My God, here I am. The floods of demons have lifted up their voices against me, like the rushing in of many waters to drown me. Because I let Anger rule me instead of having You rule over me. I am sorry. Please forgive me."

The minions try to stop Moriah from praying. "He's not going to forgive you. You've done the unpardonable sin too many times. No need to pray. You've lost. You are one of us."

In spite of all the doubts spoken to Moriah, a bluish aura manifests itself around Moriah.

The cluster of Minions and any late arrivals of Minions cannot penetrate the blue aura, and they bounce off. But they hold their wings, hands and feet together and cover up the aura all around like a blackened cloak.

They try again to influence Moriah. "You already lost girl. You are ours. We are many, and you are alone. No one can hear you. Give up."

Moriah drops on her knees to the ground. Tears stream down her face. She is close to exhaustion. She covers her face with both of her hands. And with every word she prays, golden smoke rises like incense into the heavens, and the minions are getting zapped with it.

"Lord God Most High, I am yours. Thank you for your truth and promises."

The Minions still try to stop Moriah's prayers. "Don't let her talk. Shhhh her…" The

Minions and Demons are everywhere trying to suffocate Moriah.

Moriah struggles but gets up with determination. She speaks in faith gaining strength with every word. "I am wearing the breastplate of righteousness."

In her mind's eyes, a visible armor breastplate appears around her chest.

"And a helmet of salvation." A golden helmet shields her head and face. "I am girded with truth, and my sword is the Word of God. The Bible is God's Word and my feet are bringing good news. Good news for God's people and bad news for unclean spirits and demons." Her hair hanging down from the helmet blows like in high winds. With every word she speaks, she gains more power.

"Lord, you gave us the power to tread on serpents and scorpions and over ALL the power of the enemy, and nothing shall by any means hurt us." Moriah walks in place, first slowly, then stomps every step. Little by little the darkness from the demonic world decreases.

The minions and demons squeal like a heard of pigs. "Stop her… finish her… noooo… eee…"

Moriah stands firm. "I tell you unclean spirits to let go of me. I am the property of the Most High and the Lord paid the price for me with his blood. He forgave me at the cross. Leave me in the Name of the Lord." She extends her arms and hands out toward the sky.

A burst of light and energy comes from Moriah. The remaining Minions break into thousand dark pieces like in an explosion and disintegrate. Moriah is free. She breathes deeply.

All Minions and unclean spirits vanish.

The armor fades away. Moriah's head is bowed, and her arms hang down. "Ah, thank you, Lord. Wow."

A group of four joggers passes Moriah. They look at her as if she is crazy. Moriah shrugs her shoulders, laughs, and waves. Then she walks back into the gym.

*

The people are leaving, slowly but surely. Most are disappointed because there wasn't a champion. How can there not be a champion? It was a tournament after all. And people are asking why they felt like they wanted one of the fighters to be dead. So they are leaving with a lot of unanswered questions.

Moriah sees her friends and rushes to their side.

Mr. Hanes grabs Moriah's arm. "I'm glad you're okay, girl. You had us worried. But that's my girl. You made it out all right."

Moriah gives Mr. Hanes a quick hug. "Yes, thanks for your prayers everyone. And how is Vincent?"

David shrugs his shoulders. "He's seen better days, but he looks like he is going to make it."

Diane suggests, "Let's go and get a coffee or something. My knees are shaking from what happened here today."

Moriah nods thankfully. "Yeah, coffee sounds great."

Mr. Hanes starts to roll his wheelchair. "Let's go."

Moriah grabs on to Mr. Hanes' wheelchair, and together they leave.

*

The next morning at Mr. Hanes house, everything is silent. Mr. Hanes is sipping his coffee and eating his toast while reading the Bible.

Vincent joins him. He looks rough.

Mr. Hanes glances at him. "Good Morning, Vincent. Have some coffee."

Vincent nods. "Thanks." Then he gets himself a coffee mug and pours the coffee. He drinks it black. Then he slumps down in a chair at the table.

Mr. Hanes looks up from his Bible. "Rough morning?"

Vincent is discouraged. "Rough everything. I think I have to close down the school."

Mr. Hanes is concerned. "Why? People want the school. It gives them something to look forward to."

Vincent takes another sip of his coffee. "Honestly? H. you were there, yesterday. I have no idea what happened, but I almost killed that man. And you know what? It felt almost like someone made me do it. That scared the heck out of me."

"You are right. What I saw yesterday was scary. Maybe it had something to do with your nightmares, which you have every night?"

Vincent looks at Mr. Hanes in surprise. "You know? How?"

Mr. Hanes is very careful how he answers Vincent's question. "Every night, I think you have a nightmare because I can hear your voice, with agony. It must be something terrible. Want to talk about it?"

Vincent is a little hesitant, but then he starts to talk. "It's mostly the same nightmare. I left Korea because of them. My teacher died one night in his sleep and ever since then, I was afraid that it was my fault. It's almost like these thoughts in my head tell me that I am a killer. I know that I am not a murderer, well, up until yesterday. Back then, these thoughts tried to take over, I had to get away from Korea and came back home. And I had some peace for a while. Now it all came back. I am so stuck."

Mr. Hanes waits a few moments before he tells Vincent. "It sounds to me like a supernatural evil power wants you. You know that our small group of friends has prayed for people and they are free now, even to this day. We could get together and read the Bible. Maybe the Lord will show us what's happening?"

Vincent shrugs his shoulders. He doesn't think that a bit of Bible reading and praying is going to help him. "I don't know. I think I am just going to quit everything."

"Vincent, before you do that, why not give prayer a chance. It might be the only help."

Vincent takes a big gulp of his coffee. He looks at Mr. Hanes. "Heck, yeah. I don't know what to do right now anyway. You don't think everyone hates me now?"

"No way, Vincent, everyone is for you. The Bible says our struggle is not against flesh and blood, but against principalities and powers of darkness in high places."

Mr. Hanes looks for the scripture verse in his Bible and pushes the book toward Vincent pointing out the passage.

"Read the sixth chapter of Ephesians or the whole epistle. It will tell you all about powers we don't see."

Mr. Hanes takes a bite of his toast while Vincent reads the verses. Vincent goes down the page with his index finger. "That's fantastic,

H., and a very good idea, I used to love reading the Bible, and it has been years. Thanks, H."

Mr. Hanes smiles and takes a sip of coffee. "You're a nice man Vincent, not a killer. I know this out of experience. If you want to, you can use this Bible. I have another one."

Vincent takes the Bible and fills his coffee cup again. "I'll read in my room then, H. I don't feel like going anywhere today."

Mr. Hanes nods with understanding. "Smart move Vincent. I'll call David, Moriah, and Diane to come over tonight for prayer. Will that be all right?"

Vincent scratches his head. "The sooner the better, I guess. I'd love to have a sound sleep for once. Yeah, tonight is perfect. Thanks, H." He leaves the living room, and Mr. Hanes gets busy with calling the friends.

*

The evening is here and the night is quiet as usual. The streetlights shed dim lights on the street.

David arrives with his motorcycle. He parks behind Diane's car and turns his headlight off. He looks around. Not another soul. He walks toward Mr. Hanes' front entry and rings the bell.

Diane opens the door and welcomes David with a short hug. Then she closes the door again.

Even though the street looks deserted, the spirit world is very busy. Glorious Angels of light with sparkling swords surround the house like a protective wall.

The dark side is busy as well. Black shining movement round about are closing in from the distance slithering and floating toward Mr. Hanes home. They stop at a safe distance careful not to be zapped by the light. Then they pull blindfolds over their eyes and swarm toward the Angels of light and attack them.

Most Angels of light engage in the warfare. Sparks glitter and swords clank. It seems that both sides have equal strengths. But the power of the angels of light depends on the faith and endurance of the earthlings, but if they start to doubt, the dark side gets stronger.

One Angel of light remains to protect the house. His light extends a shield around and above the house like a shiny prism curtain.

Oblivious to the battle going on in the heavenly our friends are together in Mr. Hanes' living room.

Mr. Hanes sits in his wheelchair at the table and closest to Vincent. His favorite Bible is open on the table.

Vincent moves to a cushioned chair and away from the table. "You know my story. And I feel like I have no way to turn. And thanks to H., he reminded me of my childhood faith and that I love reading the Bible. I've read the Bible most of the day today, and I don't feel so torn up on the inside anymore."

Diane puts her hand on Vincent's shoulder. "What you've told us and what's been happening to you is a big load to carry. We are your friends and don't want to see you go."

David agrees. "Don't even think about leaving us. The town needs your school. And we need you."

Vincent is touched by the words of his friends. "Thanks, guys. I like it here, but it seems like, if I get too deep into fighting, then something is trying to take over, and that's when I almost lose control, every time."

Mr. Hanes nods. "Let's get started. Don't worry Vincent it's going to go well."

Moriah scoots a chair from the table closer to Vincent. She positions it so that she is more like face to face with Vincent. "Vincent, we must establish the real power here. Tell us, what do you know about Jesus?"

Vincent shrugs his one shoulder. "I know that he is the Son of God and that everyone who calls on the name of the Lord will be saved."

Moriah smiles, "That's excellent. Now we also need to tell the spirit world what we know. And the best way to do this is to read from God's Word."

She nods at Mr. Hanes. He starts reading, "Here in the passage from Philippians 2:10 it says, that at the name of the Lord every knee should bow, of things in heaven and things on earth and things under the earth."

Everyone nods in agreement and says in unison, "Amen."

Vincent also says, "Amen. Yeah, that's powerful I always looked to God for directions in my life. Then I went to Korea, and things are so much different there. But I'm convinced that was what I was supposed to do—"

*

While our group of friends is praying inside, and establishing the power of the Lord, the Angels of Light gain strength in the fight against the forces of darkness and push them away from the house, back and further back.

*

Moriah is praying. "Lord, here we are in your Name. We lift Vincent up, and ask you to show us, what we should do."

Diane walks around the room with her eyes closed and with a fist directed toward the floor as if she sees something. She prays fervently. "Jesus, please, we need your help."

David addresses Vincent. "Vincent, did you ever forgive that man in Korea. You know the one who married your girl?"

A shadow brushes over Vincent's face. "Hell no! They should ask ME to forgive them. I won't do it."

The friends continue to pray and ignore what Vincent said. It's of crucial importance for them to find a way for Vincent to see where his personal path went wrong and invited darkness.

*

Outside the house, an Angel of Darkness wins the upper side of an Angel of Light. Their hair and garments flow like in an intense storm. Their swords clash and POW, sparks are flying. Two Supernatural beings have a head-on collision.

*

Mr. Hanes takes the lead. "Lord, thank you that you are our God. Bathe us with your light and truth that your child will be set free."

A clear blackish light appears inside the living room and slips inside Vincent's body. Right at this moment, Vincent's countenance

changes into the grimace of Warrior-Foe.
Vincent speaks with that voice. "Ha, you worms.
You think you are so smart and great to do
anything about anything. Look at you; you are
fools all of you."

Moriah sees right through the shape of
Vincent and recognizes Warrior-Foe from the
combat. "I saw you yesterday. You are the one,
who tries to hold Vincent captive. As you know,
we belong to the Lord and in His presence do we
stand. You unclean spirit must leave Vincent
this minute."

Warrior-Foe chokes Vincent's throat. But
he leaves enough air that he can talk through
Vincent. "Ba! Unclean spirit, don't make me
laugh. I am more than a spirit. I am a Warrior
and this soul here belongs to me."

*

Outside the house, the battle rages on.
The Angels of Darkness push forward and try to
overtake the Angels of Light. They are pushing
closer to the house.

*

Moriah is not easily intimidated. She keeps on asking questions. "Why should we believe you? Why would his soul belong to you?"

Warrior-Foe stops strangling Vincent. "Because, he swore himself to me and my kingdom. He is mine. Ha, and you can't do anything about it."

The friends are puzzled by these words.

Mr. Hanes gets a glimpse of truth. "Oh yeah? This must be about the ancient oath."

Moriah gets tougher. "You warrior demon, be quiet, you. I want to talk to Vincent. Vincent, listen. Vincent, snap back here. We need to know what that ancient oath is all about."

Vincent's face shimmers back until it shows no sign of Warrior-Foe's grimace. He is back in clarity and looks at his friends a little confused. "The oath? When I got my first Dan, I needed to swear: that fighting will be my only focus. There is no body or mind, only fighting, that's what life became."

Moriah tells Vincent. "Renounce it."

Vincent truly doesn't know. "How can I?"

David helps him. "God has given you a mind and a body as unique gifts. Fighting alone would destroy you and your destiny."

Mr. Hanes helps. "Say something like, I renounce the oath, and I believe fighting is only a sport, not life, focus hard."

Vincent nods with understanding. He concentrates and wants to speak, but Warrior-Foe flashes back to the surface. And both of them are struggling. Vincent tries to resist Warrior-Foe, and he tries to hinder Vincent to speak the words. Warrior-Foe flashes in and out of Vincent's body.

All the while the friends are praying in whispers or sometimes, David or Diane speak up. "Set him free."

*

The battle outside seems to be equal with a slight advantage of the Angels of Light pushing the enemy back inch by inch.

*

Moriah gets impatient with the ongoing struggle within Vincent. She charges. "I told

you to let go of Vincent. He belongs to the
Lord."

David leans over and puts his hand on
Vincent's shoulder. "Yes, you ancient spirit,
let Vincent go."

Warrior-Foe is losing his hold on Vincent.
He yields to David's hand holding Vincent's
shoulder, starting to get out of Vincent like
stretched gum, and wanting to pull into David.

Moriah sees the attack on David and yells,
"David, don't touch Vincent."

David seems already affected by the force
of Warrior-Foe and doesn't hear Moriah. With
the lower hand and fingers curled, she rams his
arm and urges. "David, get away from Vincent.
That thing tried to take you."

David comes to himself and lets go of
Vincent's shoulder. Vincent has a moment of
strength and shouts. "My life belongs to the
Lord who made heaven and earth. I renounce
anything else I swore."

Warrior-Foe wants to zap back into
Vincent, but it doesn't work. Stuck, he is half
out and half in Vincent.

Moriah ceases the moment. "Now, forgive
your enemy, Vincent."

It is hard for Vincent, but at last, he says the words. "God, I want to obey you and forgive Cho Ming. These memories hurt. Please help me and give me your grace to be able to forgive him."

Mr. Hanes shouts. "Yes. We are witnesses. Vincent renounced the ancient oath and you, unclean spirit, or whatever demon or warrior you are, must get away from our dear friend. NOW."

David is in agreement. "In the Lord's Name."

Vincent screams with Warrior-Foe's voice, "Noooooo…"

And then at once Warrior-Foe flees out of Vincent's body. The force pushes Vincent including his chair clear across the room. Vincent and the chair crash down on the floor.

Moriah still sees Warrior-Foe. "Leave this room and go back where you came from, in the name of the Lord."

Warrior-Foe looks distorted and uglier than ever. He vanishes.

Vincent gets up and holds his head. "Ouch. Is it over?" he picks up the chair.

Diane smiles at Vincent. "Yes, it's over, and you are free. God is good."

Everyone chimes in. "God is good."

Moriah gets a small bag out of her pocket. She pulls five necklaces with the Prayer Blaze Pendants out and gives each of her friends one. "Here, the promised necklace. They finally came in the mail." The friends put their necklaces on.

Moriah claps her hands and starts to sing. "Oh God, you're an awesome God, You reign from heaven above, with wisdom, power, and love, Oh God, you're an awesome God… Everyone… Oh God, you're an awesome God, you reign from heaven above with wisdom power and love, our God is an awesome God…"

While they sing, they join hands and sway their upper bodies sideways. They sing the refrain over and over again.

★

Mr. Hanes' house outside is illuminated, and bright light surrounds it. The Angels of Light rejoice. The angels of darkness shy back from the bright light and flee away.

Moriah, David, and Diane leave the house to go home. "Praise the Lord that was a successful prayer meeting," Diane says.

David waves to the girls. "Good night." He gets on his motorcycle and zooms away. The girls wave after him.

Diane gives Moriah a ride in her car.

*

The next morning, Mr. Hanes sits in his wheelchair in the doorway of his front door. He is waiting for the mailman who just arrives. "Good morning, Mr. Hanes. You look cheerful today." He hands him a bundle of mail.

Mr. Hanes takes his letters. "Thanks, George. Have a lovely day today. See you tomorrow."

George turns and goes on his way.

Mr. Hanes looks through the letters and takes out a special envelope. He drops the other ones in his lap. He opens the letter and reads it.

Putzi sits next to Mr. Hanes and is surprised when Mr. Hanes gets excited. "I'll be darned. First place! Oh my, a year's supply of birdseed. I've got to tell everyone."

Mr. Hanes is just about to wheel himself inside and calls Vincent. "Vincent! Can you come? You won't believe—"

Mr. Hanes stops in his tracks. A Van halts with Squeaky breaks in front of his house. Putzi barks and barks.

Vincent comes running to Mr. Hanes' side. He is shirtless but wears his Prayer Ablaze necklace and his Cross pendant. "Yes, H.? Try me, I can believe a lot of things, especially after yesterday. What's the TV van doing here?"

Mr. Hanes caresses Putzi's fur by the ears, and Putzi quiets down. "I don't know. Maybe they got the wrong address?"

A woman holding a microphone with the number 5 on it approaches Mr. Hanes and Vincent. She stops for a moment and looks at the cameraman behind her.

She starts to speak when he says. "Ready to roll."

The woman speaks into the microphone. "Hello, I am Cindy from News channel five. We are at Mr. Hanes house. But wait. Let me find out first. 'Are you Mr. Hanes?'"

Mr. Hanes nods. "Yes, Ma'am. What's the occasion?"

Cindy speaks on, "We heard that you won the photo contest for the Birdseed Inc. Photo competition and would like to interview you about it. Is that all right with you?"

Vincent shouts. "You Won! Congratulations."

Mr. Hanes looks at Vincent. "That's what I was just going to tell you. But how do you people know about it, when I just got the letter in the mail?"

Mr. Hanes waves the letter in his hand. And Vincent takes it and reads it. "Top notch, H.!"

Cindy from the news channel waves the cameraman to stop recording and then says to Mr. Hanes. "Mr. Hanes, it would be best if we could interview you where you took that winning photo. Would that be possible?"

Mr. Hanes is all for it. "Of course, it is possible, come, we need to go through the house to the back yard. Boy, this is so exciting."

Mr. Hanes pushes his wheelchair aside and encourages the TV team to come inside. "Come in, please."

Vincent pushes Mr. Hanes to the backyard and positions the wheelchair exactly where Mr. Hanes wants it to be. "H. I've got to put a shirt on at least. I'm sure you can handle your interview."

Mr. Hanes has a twinkle in his eyes. "You bet I can. Thanks, Vincent."

*

A crowd of students hangs out at the entrance of the martial arts school. Some look at a large sign posted on the door. It says: SCHOOL CLOSED UNTIL FURTHER NOTICE.

The students are disappointed. Anger makes his rounds among the students to find some to stir them up to get angry. He isn't very efficient.

One student shakes his head by Anger's attempt and Anger moves on to another. When Anger touches him, he lifts his shoulders and shivers.

Anger sees Alberta Gong and Doris Dim. "There we go. I've used them many times before. They get mad easily. But in a way that's boring. Oh well, better them than no one."

Hurt pops up close to Anger and startles him. "Do you need me?"

Anger raises his eyebrows mockingly. "Why should I need you? Actually yes. Could you work these earthlings over?"

Hurt salutes Anger. "Of course. Hey, they have hurt feelings already. What an easy job, quick and pain-free."

Anger cautions Hurt and points out Alberta and Doris. "Those two are mine. But it's okay if you want to work them over after they cool off."

Alberta and Doris are the closest to the door. They read the sign and are mad. Their faces turn red to purple.

Alberta Gong keeps stomping her leg on the ground. "No. That isn't right. We paid for the classes. The school needs to be open for us."

Doris agrees with Alberta. "No, it isn't right. But what are we going to do?"

Alberta huffs, "Call the police, of course."

Someone else shouts. "What are the cops going to do about it? They fight criminals, not a closed school."

The students are discouraged, sad and clueless.

One student takes a stand. "I'm going to stay right here and see if something is going to happen." He sits down on the ground with his back to the building.

Other students also sit down. One student says, "I wonder if it has something to do with yesterday's tournament. Boy, that was a heated fight. Anyone know who won the fight?"

The students around him shake their heads no. Another one speaks up. "Yeah, that was a real fight! Maybe the police shut the school down. Maybe someone died?"

The students look abhorred, hoping that no one lost his life in yesterday's battle.

Alberta looks with jealousy at the sitting students. "I wish I had a chair to sit down."

Doris remembers and says, "Oh, I have two folding lawn chairs in the trunk. Let's get them."

Alberta gets in one of the student's face. "Hey, we'll be back in a few minutes with chairs. Save us this spot, all right?"

The student nods after he recovers from Alberta's rudeness.

Alberta and Doris elbow their way through the crowd.

*

The camera man focuses his camera on the bird feeder and then to Cindy and back to Mr. Hanes. Putzi sits next to Mr. Hanes.

Vincent wears a shirt and stands there with his arms crossed. He enjoys every minute of the interview.

Cindy is talking volumes. "… Now you have seen the charming Bird feeder, folks, and I have something to give to Mr. Hanes who is the master photographer."

Mr. Hanes is surprised. "Oh?"

Cindy pulls out a check from her pocket and hands it to Mr. Hanes. He takes the paper and reads it. He raises his eyebrows and grins at Vincent. "This is a check for 500 dollars. From Birdseed Inc. Now that is cool."

Mr. Hanes holds the check up as high as he can and waves it. Vincent gets closer and looks at it.

Cindy continues into the microphone. "This is the prize money for the winning photo of Mr.

Hanes, and Birdseed Inc. will have the bird
seed delivered to you any day now. A last word
to you folks, it pays to buy bird seeds from
Birdseed Inc. because beautiful birds will come
and dine at your feeder. This is channel five
news and goodbye."

Cindy lowers the microphone, and the
cameraman takes the camera off his shoulders.
He carries it at the holder.

Mr. Hanes gets closer to Cindy. "Thank you
for doing that. Can you tell me when you will
be showing it on TV?"

"Tonight at eight o'clock on channel
five."

Putzi gets up. He wags his tail and whines
happily. He runs over to the other end of the
backyard.

Bella walks by the fence and when she sees
everyone, she stops. She greets Putzi and picks
him up and hugs him. "Oh, Putzi, I missed you
so much. You look well. Good morning Mr. Hanes.
I knocked at your front door and then I heard
voices back here."

Mr. Hanes is happy to see Bella. "Good
morning precious. I'm glad you found us. Did

you come to pick up this cute doggy? Or are you looking for Moriah?"

"Yes, Mr. Hanes, I'd like to take Putzi home. I went to the Martial Arts school, and it said it is closed."

Mr. Hanes is confused. "Did it say that? Vincent, you closed the school? I thought you changed your mind? Bella, come inside the fence please."

Bella puts Putzi down in the yard and climbs over the fence.

Cindy is interested in the development of the conversation. "The Martial arts school is closed? Wow, that's more news."

She waves the camera man to get his camera going again. Cindy points the microphone close to whoever is speaking.

Vincent admits, "The sign is there, yes. I posted it yesterday because that's what I was going to do."

Bella is brave. She takes a deep breath and shoots right out. "The thing is, my mom finally allowed me to take a class at the school. And now it's closed?"

Vincent is moved by her tender conduct. "So, I had it closed yesterday, but your friends convinced me to keep the school open. And I was thinking about it all night. I didn't have the time yet to take down the sign. We should do that right now; take the sign off and have classes."

Mr. Hanes moves his arms in Tai Chi positions with the check in the one hand. "Great idea! Can you take me?"

Bella pleads, "And could Putzi and I come also?"

Vincent spreads his arms and says joyfully. "Of course, we go together. And H. we can talk about that photography job in the car? I like photos of groups and the individual students."

Mr. Hanes agrees and pushes his wheelchair to the backyard gate. He encourages the TV team to follow. "That would be great Vincent. David wants to do all the printing. Wait till he hears about this, he'll be so excited. The blessings are showering on us. Wow."

They reach Vincent's car, and Vincent helps Mr. Hanes in. The TV crew scrambles to their van. Cindy shouts after Vincent. "We'll see you at the school then. Wait for us please."

*

Later at the Martial arts school, Vincent parks his car in front of the school. He helps Mr. Hanes out of his vehicle and into the wheelchair. Bella leaves Putzi in the car and closes the door.

David arrives with his motorcycle, and Moriah is sitting behind him. He parks next to Vincent's car. They get off the bike. Moriah hands David her helmet and walks over to Bella. They give each other a bear hug.

Moriah says softly, "Bella, you are here. I'm so glad to see you."

Bella is very happy. "I picked Putzi up from Mr. Hanes. And guess what? Vincent is here to open up the school again."

"Wow, that's great. Hi, Mr. Hanes."

The news channel five van arrives and parks right behind Vincent's car. Cindy jumps out of the van with her microphone in her hand, and the cameraman jumps out next, ready to report and film.

Cindy positions herself behind the crowd. "Now if you haven't heard, folks, the Martial

Arts School was closed. The fans are not happy at all. Look at all these people. Each and every one wants the school to open up again."

The cameraman films the students and the surrounding area. The students waiting in front of the school are upset about the closure of the school. Groups are involved in discussions, another group of eight students practice warm-ups. After filming everything, he takes the camera off his shoulders.

Vincent walks toward the entrance. Moriah pushes Mr. Hanes' wheelchair, David and Bella are right behind Moriah and the film crew walk behind David and Bella.

Alberta Gong and Doris Dim sit in their lawn chairs by the front door. They are sad because Hurt is doing a number on them, whispering into their ears.

Alberta whines, "I wish I wouldn't have been so furious at the fight."

Doris chimes in, "Me too. I don't know what came over me yesterday. I wanted to see blood."

Alberta looks intense, "I know what you mean. I had to repent of it that very same day."

"Me too."

They stop talking when the students see Vincent. Most of the students walk up to him with many questions. All the voices at once make it hard to hear a word.

Alberta gets up from her lawn chair. "What's going on over there? Can you see anything?"

Doris gets up as well and stretches her neck and then she slumps back into her chair. "No, just a lot of people. But whatever it is, we will know soon. It's moving toward us. Oh!"

Alberta shouts, "It's Vincent."

The ladies jump out of their chairs again and with lots of effort they step on top of their chairs to get a better look.

Doris points out. "Look at this over there. There's a TV crew right behind him. I know the woman from Channel 5. They have the latest news from town every day."

The cameraman stops and films the crowd from a new angle, and his camera stops at Vincent.

Vincent waves his arms to calm the students down. And they quiet down eventually. Vincent has the keys to the school in his hand

and lifts them high. "Yes, after the fearsome fight at the tournament yesterday, I was convinced that I must close the school. The Martial arts school is meant for balance, harmony, and a healthy mind. And what happened yesterday at the tournament was wrong. This school is not a school to fight for fighting's sake. My friends convinced me to keep the school open."

The crowd cheers. Diane joins her friends. She is standing next to David. Moriah, Mr. Hanes, and Bella stay away from the crowd. They don't want to be stampeded.

David calls. "Open up already. We want to get more balance."

The crowd applauds and cheers again. They chant, "Yeah. Open up, open up, open up…"

The chanting grows louder the more students join in. Happy faces all around.

Cindy holds the microphone to one of the students. "Excuse me, would you please tell us, what you think about all that?"

The young man is dressed in hip hop clothing and wears a backward hat. He turns and speaks willingly into the microphone. "Since you asked, lady, this school rocks, totally."

The girl next to him agrees and speaks into the microphone. "Yeah, it rocks totally. That school is the best thing that happened to our town in a very long time."

Another young man speaks up. "Right on. Open up; you rock. Open up; you rock…"

The crowd picks up on the new slogan. "Open up, you rock. Open up, you rock…"

Vincent rips the closed sign off and tears it in half. Then he unlocks the door. The students stream happily inside.

Cindy from the news channel speaks into her microphone, and the cameraman focuses on the students running into the building. "Here you have it. Our lovely town has the rocking Martial Arts School back. I might just go in right now and sign up for a class or two for myself. This is Cindy, Channel five, and have a good night.

She signals the cameraman to cut and hands him her microphone. She also enters the Martial Arts School.

Moriah, Mr. Hanes, and Bella look at each other and laugh. They are waiting for the crowd to disperse.

Cho Ming comes around the corner.

Vincent still stands by the door. They look at each other. Cho Ming holds a photo in his hand and gives it to Vincent. Vincent takes it and stares at it for a while. It is a current picture of Cho Ming and his wife, a baby and another nice looking female. Vincent smiles.

Cho Ming speaks in Korean and tells Vincent that he is sorry. "Mian-hamnida." He squeezes Vincent's hand. "I want you to have this photo of our family. My wife says you are her best friend. She is very fond of you."

Vincent is touched, and his eyes tear up. "Oh. She said that? I am also so very sorry about yesterday. You got a good looking family."

Cho Ming smiles. He points at the photo. "This is my sister. She is single and doesn't have an arranged marriage."

Vincent laughs out loud and slaps Cho Ming's shoulder. "I don't want to mess with your traditions. The memory of losing Jasmine still hurts. However, you are all welcome to visit the States."

Cho Ming bows slightly and thanks Vincent in Korean. "Gomawa."

Vincent bows as well and thanks Cho Ming in Korean, and says, "Goodbye, go in peace. - Annyung-hi gaseyo."

Cho Ming looks at Vincent and raises his eyebrows. "Friends?"

Vincent nods, "Friends."

They smile at each other and shake hands. Then they bow down long and low in reverence.

Cho Ming replies Vincent's 'goodbye and go in peace in Korean.' "Annyung-hi gaseyo."

Vincent sighs. "Goodbye, Cho Ming. Please say hello to Jasmine. She looks very happy."

"I will. It was a good fight."

"Yes, it was. Peace be with you."

They bow again toward each other and Cho Ming leaves.

Vincent looks at him with a smile on his face. Then he walks into the school.

Moriah, Mr. Hanes, and Bella witnessed the whole spiel. Satisfied they also make their way to the doors.

Mr. Hanes comments. "Mission accomplished. Let's go and make strong fists."

Rosina comes running from down the street. She approaches fast. Her hair is shiny and combed. She smiles, and her face shows no trace of worry.

Bella sees her and runs toward her. She hugs her waist. "Mom, you are here…! Putzi is in the car, and he was so happy to see me."

Rosina waves hello to Moriah and Mr. Hanes. "I'm glad, honey. I came to sign you up for the class you want to take."

"Thanks, Mom."

Rosina walks along side with Moriah. "Moriah, thank you for being there when we needed you. And my husband thanks you too. He is doing so much better."

Moriah touches Rosina's arm. "I'm glad to hear it. And you are so welcome." Moriah pulls a necklace with the blaze prayer pendant out of her pocket and gives it to Rosina.

Rosina takes it happily and puts it around her neck. "I love this necklace, thanks. And thank you, Mr. Hanes, for taking care of Putzi."

Mr. Hanes tells Rosina. "Putzi is such a sweet dog. If you ever go out of town, I would love to take care of him."

"Thanks."

Diane peeks out of the door. "What's taking you so long? Come in already."

Bella pulls her mother by her hand. "Let's go in, Mom."

*

Down in hell Lucifer is steaming. He hasn't been mad like this for a long time, or that he can remember. Yes, boredom is usually his companion, but not at this time. He is mad as ever.

The walls shake and crumble. The demons hide. Sizzles and fizzes are everywhere.

Warrior-Foe appears before Lucifer in defiance. Lucifer is annoyed to see him. "What are you doing here? Do you dare to come here? You lost—"

Warrior-Foe interrupts Lucifer. "Says who? Everyone down here has the best example of losing, and that example is...? YOU. Remember way back when you tried to build your throne above the Creator. I once believed you, and so did a third of other Angels, which now also lost the light."

Lucifer tries to wipe away the truth of
this. "Bah! That was your choice and everyone
else's. Greed got you. You wanted more than you
had been given. And this time, what about your
big words of getting the job done?"

Warrior-Foe answers in arrogance. "Let's
say, either way, it is what it is. There will
be others I can win over to me and best without
you and your helpers."

Lucifer starts a tantrum. "Get out of my
sight."

Warrior-Foe grins hideously. "With
loathing pleasure."

Lucifer throws fireballs at Warrior-Foe,
but he vanishes before they can hit him.

Hurt, Rage, and Anger hide behind a
corner. Rage pushes Hurt, and he tumbles out of
hiding. Lucifer sees Hurt, who wants to flee.
Now Lucifer throws fire tentacles and ropes
Hurt with them. He pulls him closer. "Hurt!
They say you left, just when they needed you
for reinforcement."

Hurt whimpers. "I was… hurt. But…"

Lucifer hollers. "You ARE Hurt. That's
what you are…"

Hurt asks cautiously. "Your Highness, did they forget to tell you, that I came back and was the last one there? And none of them stayed as long as I did?"

Anger and Rage get puffed up in their hiding place. They whisper to one another. Rage asks first. "Can you believe that ugly weasel?"

Anger shakes his head. "He isn't going to change. Every time we are not around, he tries to cheat us out of our success."

Lucifer loathes Hurt, and he shows it. "Is that so? And why are you down here at such a critical time and not up there?"

Hurt steps cowardly backward. "The earthlings all got ha..ha..happy- OUCH and my work was done."

Lucifer hollers. "Out you. Get away." He throws fire, smoke, and rocks. Hurt flees into the tunnel he came out of and almost runs Rage and Anger over. They grab him and hold him tight.

Rage spits. "Watch it you weasel. Now you are not so big. Are you?"

Anger joins with Rage. "Yeah, let's get him and tear him to pieces."

Hurt frees himself and runs away from Rage and Anger as fast as he can and out of hell.

*

It is early in the morning. The promise of a gorgeous day is on the horizon.

Moriah jogs and listens to her music. She stops at her favorite bench and inhales the air deeply. She sits down and takes out the earpieces. The birds are waking up and chirp lovely.

Moriah takes out her notebook and writes. "This assignment was to save Vincent from the claws of death. And other people found salvation in the process. The enemy is defeated once again."

Moriah puts her notebook back into her pocket. Then she spreads out her arms and faces the sky. "Thank you, Lord. I can smell and feel your freedom." She takes a few steps and stops again. "I hope I learned my lesson, please help me to look to you and not what the situation seems to be, or what the people may do or look like on the outside. Until next time you need me, I'll be enjoying every minute of peace."

Moriah puts her earpieces back on and continues
jogging.
The End.

Made in the USA
Columbia, SC
03 July 2017